Tiger
Work

Also by Ben Okri

Fiction

The Famished Road
The Freedom Artist
A Prayer for the Living
Every Leaf a Hallelujah
Astonishing the Gods
The Last Gift of the Master Artists
Dangerous Love

Essays

The Mystery Feast: Thoughts on Storytelling

Poetry

A Fire in My Head: Poems for the Dawn

Tiger Work

Stories, Essays and Poems

About Climate Change

BEN OKRI

Other Press
New York

Poems, stories and essays in this book first appeared in the following: "Thirst, Knowledge and Love," *Kulturaustausch*, 2022; "The Broken," part of Writers Rebel event for Extinction Rebellion, London 2021; "And Peace Shall Return," *Emergence*, 2020; "Tiger Work," part of Writers Rebel event for Extinction Rebellion, London 2020; "The House Below," *Concrete & Ink*, 2021; "The Songbird's Silence," *Financial Times*, 2020; "Letter to the Earth," *Letters to the Earth: Writing to a Planet in Crisis*, William Collins, 2019; "Kerze," exhibition notes, Kerze, Gavin Turk, 2022; "After the End," *Emergence*, 2022; "A Short Interview," *Africa Review*, 2021; "Existential Creativity," *The Guardian*, 2021; "The Secret Source," *The New Yorker*, September 2022

1 3 5 7 9 10 8 6 4 2

Library of Congress Cataloging-in-Publication Data
Names: Okri, Ben, author.
Title: Tiger work : stories, essays and poems about climate change / Ben Okri.
Description: New York : Other Press, [2023]
Identifiers: LCCN 2023007501 (print) | LCCN 2023007502 (ebook) | ISBN 9781635423365 (hardcover) | ISBN 9781635423372 (ebook)
Subjects: LCSH: Climatic changes—Literary collections. | LCGFT: Poetry. | Fables. | Essays.
Classification: LCC PR9387.9.O394 T54 2023 (print) | LCC PR9387.9.O394 (ebook) | DDC 828/.914—dc23/eng/20230323
LC record available at https://lccn.loc.gov/2023007501
LC ebook record available at https://lccn.loc.gov/2023007502

CONTENTS

For those who love the world enough to fight for it.

"Tyger, Tyger, burning bright…"

William Blake

Read slowly

THREE PARABLES
ABOUT WATER

1

THIRST

One day a woman had come to see him because she had written to him a few times and he had never replied. They sat on his sofa while she gazed at him.

"Why haven't you written to me?"

He looked at her.

"I came all this way to see you."

"What is it you want?"

"To be your friend."

"Do you think it's possible?"

"Why shouldn't it be?"

He looked away.

"It's just you don't say anything."

He looked at her again, mutely.

"Your silence drives one crazy."

At last he spoke.

"Friendship means everything to me. I can't do it lightly anymore. It's like entrusting someone with your heart." He paused. "If I ripped out my heart and gave it to you to look after, could you?"

He made a ripping motion and presented his heart to her. She stared at his hand.

"That's scary."

"I know."

"Would you do it for me?" she asked.

"With my life, if you were my friend."

"Do you have many friends?"

"No."

"I see."

He smiled.

"My mother told me a story about a lonely prince. Being a prince made it hard for him to find true friends. He asked a wise man for help. The wise man said, 'Find out which of your friends, using only their hands, can carry water a long way from the river, without spilling it...' She didn't finish the story."

"What did she mean?"

"I'm not sure."

"I'd like to try it."

"Really? Now?"

"Do you have a bucket?"

"Yes."

"Fill it with water and let's go outside. I'll be at one end of the canal and you'll be halfway down. First I'll see if I can bring you water with my naked hands. Then you'll try."

"Do I have to?"

"Yes, this is about your requirement for friendship. I want to meet it."

"But it's not your requirement. It's mine. You must have your own."

"I'm not as wise as your mother. I will adopt yours."

He got up and fetched water in a bucket. They went out of the house and down the canal.

They found a spot where she could stand. He went off a good distance, till she waved him to stop. A moment later she was walking towards him hurriedly. When she got to him there was a small quantity of water left in her cupped hands.

"What do you want to do with it?"

"Let's pretend I'm dying of thirst, and you've brought this for me."

She lifted her hands to his face, and he drank. Then it was his turn.

When he was a child his mother had taught him how to cup his hands so that water would not escape.

"You never know when only a few drops of water will save someone's life," his mother had said.

He walked over to the bucket, halfway down the street. When he got there, he cupped his palms and scooped up some water. Then he walked towards the woman. The world shimmered like mirages in a desert. The buildings and the cars and the road were gone. There was only the woman, dying of thirst. He didn't hurry. His mother had told him to be calm in these situations. He walked steadily. Not a drop leaked from his hands. Neighbors were struck by his trancelike state. Cars went past him. Sweat ran into his eyes, but he did not blink. Then he was before her. She lowered her face and drank. The water seemed to have no end. She drank till her thirst was thoroughly quenched. She saw there was still water left in his hands.

"Have you finished?"

"Yes."

He drank the rest.

"Where did you learn to do that?"

"What?"

"Keep water running through your hands?"

"It was your thirst."

"What about it?"

"It was a great thirst. You made the little that I brought into a lot."

"I was thirsty. You took your time. I could have died by the time you got to me."

"I could have rushed and brought you nothing."

"You have no idea how hot it was. Like the desert."

"Do you know the desert?"

"Yes," she said, looking around.

2

KNOWLEDGE

The hall was packed. People had been speculating about the talk for weeks. Never before had the university invited such a person to address the academic community. The dean of faculties had hoped, in these atheistic times, that an outsider might provoke a useful debate about the state of knowledge in the world.

When she turned up the dean was surprised that she was younger than he expected. She looked worryingly young. What if her talk were a total disaster? He would be made to look a fool and might be stripped of his position.

But the moment had arrived. He made the most non-committal of introductions and fled the stage. The speaker had made only one request. She did not want a lectern. She wanted only a table with a bowl of water and a transparent glass.

She stepped forth and cast her eyes over the people in the hall. Contempt was written on many faces. The mood was thick with doubt and even a discernible mockery. She smiled.

"Can everyone see me?" she asked.

Someone gave a snorting laugh. Otherwise a dull sound of assent traveled across the hall.

"Good," she said. "Then you can't complain afterwards."

She held up the bowl of water as if to perform a miracle. Then she poured water from the bowl into the glass. Water spilled from the glass as from a gushing tap. There seemed no end to the water in the bowl. Water ran from the glass, to the table and down to the floor. Soon water covered the whole surface of the floor. No one in the audience spoke.

*

They watched first with amusement at her patent stupidity, then with surprise, and finally with alarm. The water spread along the floor and crept towards the wainscoting. There were electrical sockets at floor level. Those in the front seats lifted their feet from the ground. With a serene expression on her face, she went on pouring.

At last a man with a rough beard, from the philosophy department, could bear it no longer.

"For God's sake, woman," he shouted, "can't you see that you are flooding the room?"

At that moment the woman stopped. Something cleared in the air.

"What flooding?" she asked.

The floor about her feet was dry. She put the bowl down, and drank the water in the glass. She stared at the hall that was crowded with the best brains in the academic world. There was incomprehension and thinly veiled wonder on their faces.

She bowed and left the stage. Tremendous applause erupted behind her.

She went through the door, out of the university, and never returned.

The dean who had invited her became master of the college, and two years later was knighted for services to education.

3

LOVE

When I was a kid I used to talk to the river in my hometown.

"How are you?" I once asked.

"Not so good."

"Why not?"

"There was a time when your people used to worship me as a goddess. Back then my water was clean and pure and children loved playing in me and beautiful young girls came to fetch water. The town used to celebrate and make songs about me every year. I was quite a river back then."

"What happened? You're really tiny now."

"The factories came and began dumping things in me. I grew sluggish and the mermaids didn't come anymore to play on my shores. The town stopped making songs about me. Then they forgot about me altogether."

"I haven't. You're still my friend."

"That's why I'm still here. But I'm moving away. I only delayed going because I was waiting for you to grow up."

"Where are you going?"

"Does it matter? When you've been a goddess you don't want to be a puddle, which is what I am."

"But I'll miss you."

"When you think of your childhood in this forgetful town, you will at least always remember me as a real river. I want to leave when that memory is still fresh in one person's mind."

"I'm really sorry to hear it. Tell me where you're going so I can come and visit you."

"I'm going to be free. If something is there, your people take it for granted. They respect things that are not there anymore. They make religions out of them. When your people take something for granted, they do terrible things."

"Like what?"

"They empty their sewers into it. This they call appreciation. It is better for your people if things are no longer there."

"Is that why you're leaving, because you're not properly honored? If that's the case, I could…"

"Things only stay because they're loved. I can't bear indifference. It's the cause of all I have suffered, all the toxic waste dumped in me. No one hates me. It's just that they don't care."

The river was silent for a while.

"This is the last time you'll see me. Our fates are linked. When I'm gone you will never return."

"Why is that?"

"One day your mother and father will pass away. Then what will be left? Just the sense that no one cares about you. I am the only one that could cradle you as I did when you were a child. When I disappear, this town will die."

I never heard the voice of the river again. I grew up and traveled into the world. The last time I was back, the river had gone. The town had shrunk.

I still seek that river everywhere I go.

THE BROKEN

1

When they asked me
To come up with
Words that could speak
To a world on the verge
Of environmental collapse,
I had a crisis of my own.
Fever runs in the veins
The seasons run on broken groves.

The facts are horrific
The evidence overwhelming
And still we carry on
As if no crisis were looming.
Thunder hovers above our roofs
Earth shakes beneath our floors.

What can one say to those
Who either don't want to
Hear, or have heard enough?
What can one say
That doesn't paralyze some
With the sheer scale
Of the problem?

In the end I wrote a poem of two lines
Composed of just twelve words.
The words were photosynthesized
On grass grown on hessian
And floated on the brown river.

Can't you hear the future weeping?
Our love must save the world

Good Thames, glide gently while I sing this song
Good Thames, we know not for the earth how long

2

This earth that we
Love is in grave danger
Because of us.
We have raped,
Exploited,
Abused, wrecked.
Disemboweled
And destroyed her
We blow her up, we blast
Her apart. We smash her.
We detonate
Atomic bombs on her.
We poison her.
The oceans are acidic

The rising mouths of the sea
Will devour
Men on their lunch breaks
Women at their desks
Children wandering home
From school.
Fumes in the air
Chemicals in the water
Greenhouse emissions,
Throttling time.
Leaking landfills
Batteries and plastic
Hydrocarbons
And cows and sterile
Yields of crops
Will kill millions.
Trees are disappearing.
Forests are becoming legends,
Rare as unicorns.
All over the world
Forests have become
Graveyards of trees.
Nothing there
But the ghosts
And stumps
Of the thousand species.
The earth's topsoil
Blown away
Turned to dust
Drained and weakened.
And now trees

Have no great depths
To bind their roots
And the sudden storms
Blow over ancient oaks
And sequoias.
Saplings having thin
Earth to grow on
Are pale as blonde spiders.
Fishes are dwindling in the sea.
Can you hear the future weeping?

3

In the past we have used fear.
The awakening permafrost
The ice mountains
Of the Antarctic
Will dissolve
And drown our cities.
Deserts will roam
The world at will.
Winters will turn
To blistering summers
And summers will
Turn into hell.
Buckets will find
No water in the well.
Dolphins will perish

On our beaches.
And the ruined ships
That are grounded whales
Will be the common
Sight of our shores.

We have thrown at people
Distressing facts,
Numbers, temperatures,
Loss of species.
Will undersea
Hydrates collapse?
Will the bat and the rhino
Survive? Will the tiger
And the butterfly
Breathe the same air?
Will the fortunes
Of the songbird
Revive? Year by year
Pollination slows down
And insects, little angels,
Grow small in number.
And still we drive
Our fossil fuel cars,
Make flights
Around the world
And consume vast
Amounts of energy.
The car and the aeroplane
Ships and long haulage trucks
The lighting of cities

Buildings alight at night—
It seems to be asking
Too much of us
To alter how we live
So that life on
Earth can survive.

Facts don't alter our dreams
Or change our minds.
We can't retrace the track
From the cave to spaceships.
We can't undo the air conditioner
Or the computer.
Can't walk backwards
From space stations
To the club or spear
From the oven
Back to the boomerang.
Nobody wants to turn
Back civilization's
Clock. No one wants
To regress. Fear
Doesn't work.
And guilt doesn't work.
The man who kills
The lion would long
Have closed his heart.

So I thought that maybe
Love could shift our vision
Shift our breath

Shift our dreams
See the far as near
Faraway desert in
The exhaust of a car
Flowering oasis
In the solar panel.
With fear we act
Hastily and unsteadily.
Tear up a friendship
In a chemical mood
Destroy a lifetime's love
In a manner that's rude
Lose a future
Close up a past
Brick up the present
So nothing may last.
With love we act wisely,
And comprehensively.
Hold our breath
And wait for the madness
To pass
Let the seed show
What acres it may grow.

Maybe if we all do
Something modest
Then the dead land
Can yield roses again
And desert be fertilized
With marigolds.
Then real change can

Be accomplished.
Maybe it's not
A going back.
Not a return to the serenity
Of the plough
Or the switch-led bullock
Or walking across the valley
To the remote school
Or fetching water
In a perforated calabash
From a broken river.
Maybe it's a going forward,
Living in harmony
With ourselves and the world.
Watching the fruit tree bloom
In the quiet season
Drinking the clear water
After the long walk
Listening to the flowers
Furl in the moonlight
Working in the garden
With sunlight and music
Fructifying time
Rewilding our dreams.
Maybe living simply
Is the evolutionary way.

Perhaps we've grown
Far too complicated
For our own good.
Want our fruits to ripen

Without much time
Desire the mango and the banana
Out of season
Out of rhyme
Want all the nice
Things of the world
Without paying the price
Technology without
Despoliation
Jewelry without
Exploitation
Latest fashion
Without sweatshops
Living like kings and queens
With faraway peoples
As invisible slaves
To sit on top of the world
With a humming conscience
While colonialism morphs,
And acquires a smooth voice,
A caring demeanor,
Seems to make sense,
But has the same
Deadly effect.
We want more than
We need.

Kind Yangtze, glide smoothly while I sing this song
Kind Yangtze, we know not for the earth how long

4

I think that love
Is the highest
Economy of life.
It moves the world
With an invisible touch.
And the labors of Hercules
Don't seem so much.
For money we slave
And we plot and we kill
We sweat in the desert
And freeze in the office.
But with love we give gifts
Beyond the cost of life
Never-ending gifts
That transcend time's strife.
It is the most
Efficient force
For civilization.
Symmetry in the garden
And the dream of music.
If we woke up
To our love for
The earth
We'd stop doing
Most of the things
We are doing.

No more plastic into the sea
No more hybrids into the earth.

In the Tao Te Ching
There's a light-crammed
Passage which says
That the sage loves
The world as they love their body.
If the earth were our body
Would we do half the things
To it that we're doing?
Take a nuclear blast
To the kidney
Smash the heart
With metal spikes
Frack the intestines
Mine the brain
With explosive rain.

Nothing can save
Our world but love.
Contemplating
The beauty of the leaf
Meditating
On the breathing
Of a child
Or cradling in one's arm
The face the dream.

For love is the last power
That stands between
Us and extinction.

Old Ganga, glide sweetly while I sing this song
Old Ganga, we know not for the earth how long

5

For when we act
With love
We act with all
The great powers
Of the human spirit.
The mother who raises
The car to free her child
The father who labors
From dawn to dawn
No other quality
Comes close
To bringing out
The full genius
Of the human race.

Toughness will fail.
Even the nail
Succumbs to rust.
And will exhausts
Itself in the end.
Armies march to the edge
Of the world
And still the war remains.
Only love is cosmic.
The stars, the heart.
Only love is endless.

6

What we need now
In this eleventh hour
When the bell tolls
From the sinister tower
Is the greatness
Of the human.
Gilgamesh in the form
Of a child.

This is the time
To show that we
Are greater than
Our history, our
Education,
Greater than all
The brainwashing
That makes us feel
That we can't be
Agents of change.
So I went out into
The streets today
And marched with millions
To light a way
So I said to the armies
Return to the hearth.
Even a child can
Change the day
Even you can
Make a new way.

The greatness we
Need is love. There's
No true greatness
without this love.
Enkidu is with us
Even as he falls.
Sango is with us
In his darkened cell.

When we love we
Know the right thing to do.
We will divert the river
Through our murky hearts
We will cleanse the wasteland
With our hands and carts.

I'm not here
To prescribe
This or that action—
"Take out the compost."
"Put a solar panel
On that sloping roof."
"Don't drive a car."
"Don't fly if
It's not far."
"Don't waste water."

Do you love
This world?
Seas, valleys,
Trees, destinies,

Coral reefs?
Do you love
This earth?
Faces, bodies,
Dreams, hollies?
Then all
You have
To do
Is listen to
Your love.
What did she whisper
By the stream
What did that
Look of his mean?
Don't do to
The earth
What you
Won't do
To your body.
Don't detonate
Nuclear bombs
In the heart
Don't frack
The eyes
Don't mine
The genitals
With metal files.

Great Nile, run bravely while I sing my song
Great Nile, we know not for the world how long

7

But the love I'm
Talking about
Is not passive.
Doesn't sleep
When the baby
Cries on the hot bed
Doesn't stare
With placid eyes
When a lion
Crouches near.
It is a love that acts
That roars
At the crouching
Shadow
Of tower or power
Of the minister
Who lets the rivers
Turn into sewers.
It is active.
It is a love that stops
Something awful
Happening to
The one you love.
It's protective.
I went out into
The dark today
And fought to stop
The forest

From falling away.
I raised the alarm
At the fires
In the farm.

Let's turn
The fierce
Force of
Our love
To saving life
On this planet.
March and sing
And do the tough thing
Demand climate justice
That those who cause
The greater climate damage
Bear the higher cost.
Should the tortoise
Bear the same weight
As the elephant?

Save the earth one
Step at a time.
It's time we began.
Do it now,
In whatever way
You can.

What is love's most
Magical quality?
It inspires

Transformation.
The men who killed
Half the earth
Became its
Greatest warriors.
The most indifferent
Into the most passionate.
The hater becomes
A lover
The denier
An elaborator.

Love changes us.
Changes stone
And rust
Dead land
And dust.

Will Gilgamesh
Cut down the trees?
Can the domestic cat
Become a lioness?
Can the rat become
A tiger, or the bat
A glimmering unicorn?
Will Humbaba
Defend forests?
Can *Homo sapiens* leap
Into something higher
Not superman
But transcendent being?

Can we become
Something more
Needing a new name?

We have
Got to achieve
That rare
Thing, a
Quantum
Leap in our
Life's possibilities.

From devouring
The earth
To making a world;
From waste
To conservation;
From pollution
To transmutation.

Everything we need
Is here, sun, sea,
Earth, wind,
Imagination, will,
Vision, love, mind.

We need
To leap
Right now
To the next stage
Of our evolution.

Maybe this was
The only way we were
Going to get there.
Through the dead end
And the climate terminus
The follies in the garden.
Maybe we're only
Forced to make this leap
Because we've nowhere
Else to go
We've run out
Of road
And instead
Of tipping over
Into our own abyss
We do the unthinkable
And leap to the next stage
Of the human.
In the dying minutes
Of our millennial drama.

Without
This leap
There's no
Future.

It's too late
To stroll
To the next
Stage. Too
Late to let

It happen
Organically.
Too late
To let nature
Take its course.

In that
Sense, we
Are at
A terminal
Moment.

At no other
Time has the world
Depended on us
On what we do
Or don't do.

The trees look
At us
And wonder
Dogs regard
Us with
Quizzical eyes
Newborn
Babies stare
At us and
Mutely ask
If we know
What we're
Doing.

The future
Pauses
At the gasoline
Station
Waiting for
A lift
To itself.
The past
Looks forward
At us
And recoils
At the consequences
Of itself.
The present
Waits coiled
Between
Abyss
And the
Unknown.

It is either
Death or
Transformation.
It is either
Extinction or
Becoming a
Newer,
More efficient
Species.

Will the bees
In the garden
Pollinate?
Will the seed
Unfurl
Into new
Flowers?
Will we harness
The mycelium
Realm, create networks
To the future?
Will the dance
In the garden
Levitate?
Will the smoke
Light
Its own fire?
Will the end
Of time
Be the beginning
Of a new
World?
Will we
Bequeath
To the ages
A transcendent
Light?
Will our cars
Sail through
The air
With the power

Of our thought?
Will the new energy
Of the future
Be spiritual?
Will we power
Our homes
With the orgasm?
Will the planes
Sail through
The air with
The collective
Electricity
Of passengers?
Will we discover
The infinite
Source
Of energy
That was always
There,
Within us
In the eternal
Substances
Of the air
And light?
Isn't it time
For that
Unexpected
Flight?

Nothing
Ordinary
Can achieve this.

Only love can do it.

Can't you
Hear the
Future
Weeping?

Our love
Must save
The world.

AND PEACE SHALL RETURN

Once upon a time there was a planet with vast seas, polar regions, abundant forests, and splendid continents.

Its civilization had evolved from the age of stone to the age of artificial intelligence.

Those who lived on the planet thought that no matter what they did life would continue. In less than ten thousand years, they transformed their societies from rough conditions to ways of life so sophisticated that everything they did directly or indirectly contributed to the death of their planet and to their own annihilation.

They had ample evidence of the daily destruction they were wreaking on themselves and on their environment, but they did not heed it.

They fell into the "invisible effects" fallacy. This holds that though we do things which add up to a catastrophe, we are unable from moment to moment to see the effect of our actions. And because we don't see the effect from moment to moment, we therefore think that there isn't an effect.

This blindness enabled people to continue their suicidal relationship with the earth right up to the very last moment.

*

According to our calculations, the earth has been silent now for twenty thousand years. It is at last showing signs of the regeneration of its forests and its seas after its utter destruction.

On our journey across the earth we came upon scattered notes and half-worked stories left behind by the last human beings in the very twilight of their history.

It seems that their gods died a long time ago. Then towards the end, they declared the final death of God and ascended the throne. The results are unedifying. These notes show that it is easier to kill off gods or dethrone them than it is to be one.

What is strange is that in their last days they carried on exactly as they had done over their final decades. They altered nothing in their lives to try to avert the disaster that they saw coming and which was evident every day.

What destroyed them ultimately was not some momentous event, the collision of asteroids, the drowning of their cities, the poisoning of their air, the detonation of nuclear bombs. The suicide of humanity was in their mesmerism. They were chained to the past.

It was also in their fatalism. They accepted, for centuries, that they were fundamentally unable to change. They were unable to create a new future.

In this they were consistent. They were killing themselves little by little every day and it didn't seem to trouble them.

Of all the tragic stories of vanished species we encountered across the innumerable galaxies, theirs was the most unheroic.

THE LAST SOLITUDE

*The first story was found in a half-submerged house in a city
that was once so flooded only spires remained visible above
the waterline. We surmise that over the next three thousand
years the waters receded, as the earth, with its unerring in-
stincts, rebalanced itself in a world without humans.*

*The manuscript was found intact, with some pages
missing. It showed no evidence of having suffered from
being submerged. Perhaps some members of the species had
perfected the art of writing on a kind of paper that resisted
water erosion.*

*

Today I woke late and observed the light fading early into
the darkness. I spend my days reading. On the television it
seems the masters of the earth have won complete control
of the world. Everywhere they have gained power. They
now form one unified chain of control across the main cen-
ters of the Western world. They control the news channels,
most of the newspapers, and have penetrated our digital
life and spy on our every move and listen in on our every
conversation. And how did I vote in the last election? Did
I vote against their candidate? Did I vote for the other can-
didate who wanted to make modern life more transparent
and had a good program for the environment? No. And

why not? Well, all the newspapers made any alternative sound like the end of the world. They frightened me. So I voted with my fear. Afterwards I regretted it. But if it were to happen again, they would get to me again. I now accept that I am a prisoner of something, but I don't know what it is.

I wake up and drink green tea and go to the gym. I work out to keep my body fit and my weight down. I starve through the day. I rigorously monitor my calorie intake. I do a little yoga and breathe deeply by the window.

I also breathe in the daily death of the world. I try to avoid the news. It seems to me now that every news item brings me closer to death. I don't think they mean to, but every story they report seems to help us die a little. Sometimes it is death by hopelessness. Other times it is death by despair, or indifference, or obsession.

For a hundred years now, they have been saying there are too many people on the planet. At night I cannot sleep. I wonder where we will fit all the people on the limited space of this earth. In my dreams I sometimes see them crowding over me, standing side by side with nowhere to move and no air to breathe. I eat less each day because I fear that there won't be enough food to go round. I am aware that this does not help the situation one bit, but I can't help it.

I work at home. There are days when I do not speak to another human being. I find human beings frightening. I think that they are the most frightening things in the whole world. They are scarier than cancer, disease, wild animals, ghosts, or monsters. I can't think of anything scarier than us.

The world existed for hundreds of thousands of years before we came along. Then we evolved and created civilizations, and in the last hundred years we have done more to destroy our habitat than malevolent aliens could ever have done to us.

You meet a human being and they seem normal and fine and even quite harmless. But all the evil in the world has come from humans. It didn't come from anywhere else. We hate our own kind and would leave them to die if they threatened us. We hate those who are different from us and would get rid of them if they intimidated us in any way.

We have eaten this planet to extinction. I joined an organization to help save the earth not that long ago, but found many of the people so quietly obnoxious and judgmental that they seemed to me part of the problem too.

Now when I meet human beings, something in me flinches. I do not know who I am meeting. I do not know their heart. People frighten me because of the things they passively allow to happen, the things they turn a blind eye to, the things they can't be bothered to care about. We should be the blessing of the planet, should add our beauty to the earth's beauty. But all we have done is add pollution, and waste, and evil, and destruction.

We make filth everywhere with our aspirations. Everest was pristine till, with our ambition for conquest, we turned those rare heights into one of the dustbins of the world. Dolphins gag on our plastic waste. Sea turtles choke on it. The radioactive stuff we have accumulated will be toxic for thousands of years after we have vacated the earth. Day by day we believe in less and less.

My father had nothing to teach me about life except getting ahead and putting myself first. I grew up in the aridity of that philosophy. Then a day came when I had no reason to go on living. I did not care enough about looking after myself, and it got too stressful living only to get ahead.

It was exhausting always trying to be number one. I had doubts about referring to myself that way. Why should I put myself ahead of others? Isn't that what everyone else is doing, making the world a constant battleground between individuals, states, races, religions, classes, genders? We are raised with war in our hearts, with war at the depth of our dreams. And war is what we reap every day.

I watched my father grow old in the dryness of his philosophy. Nothing flowered in him. His insight didn't get richer. He said the same things at eighty that he had said at thirty-five. He seemed to have learned little in his long sojourn on this planet.

I think the philosophy we are living by is choking the life out of us. We are now barely alive as people. This is perhaps why it is easier for us to spread death in our politics and our foreign policies.

I watch the world every day and wonder what went wrong with those fine dreams that the race had in its infancy. We have overcomplicated ourselves. I have more allergies now than I had when I was a child. There are more sicknesses around, more than there ever were fifty years ago. Where are they coming from?

We are proliferating disease and illness. I think it is nature's revenge for strangling her, for tampering with her, and for being divorced from her. We are isolated and rootless in our lack of belief in anything. Our world is ripe only for rapists and serial killers and mass murderers and the murderers of children in their schools and people in their mosques and churches. The murder at the heart of our culture has been unknowingly sanctioned by our philosophy.

Meanwhile we refine our food and our tastes, we kill ourselves trying to join the rich 1 percent, and we despise the poor. And if we are poor ourselves, we live without hope, in council estates, succumbing to the consolation of drugs and too many children.

It's why I decided not to have children. Whenever I see a child, I can't stop myself crying afterwards. I love them so much. There's nothing I want more than a child.

We human beings have abdicated the responsibility of being human. We claim the status of gods without being as wise as horses or as intelligent as flowers. Our bloated egos make us stupid. How can one entrust a child to such a species? How can I bring such a precious being into—

CHILDREN'S GAMES

This one was found in a house in a big city, among the pages of a disintegrating book.

*

My daughter came home from nursery today and wanted to share the song she had learned that morning. It was evening and we were in the living room, my husband and I. He

47

was trying to read, but a persistent drill somewhere outside kept making him look up. Then our daughter bounded into the living room and said:

"Shall I tell you what I learned today?"

"Yes," I said, thinking it was time for her to be in bed. It was nine o'clock, and still she showed no signs of slowing down.

"Okay," she said, bright as a bell. She's only three and has the linguistic skills of a six-year-old and more imagination than one thinks possible. Sometimes with terror I look upon her and wonder if she's a genius who's been born to us, some kind of freak of the mind, the blessing and the judgment of a new generation, whom we have brought forth at the most perilous time in the history of the world.

"I'll be the teacher and you the student," she said, and my husband and I exchanged glances. It is like this every day. Each new day she does something strange and unusually intelligent for her age, and sometimes she says something that makes us wonder if it isn't a god speaking through her.

"All right," my husband and I said.

Then she held a rattle in her hand. It was a blue rattle. She was smiling. She shook the rattle and started to sing. She sang with a curious smile on her face, as if she knew what she was doing, as if there was going to be a twist in it, and we had no choice but to follow.

"What's your name?" she asked her father.

"Daddy," he said.

"Daddy came to school today,
Daddy came to school today,
Daddy came to school today."

She sang the same song for me, for Mummy. She looked around and saw a favorite doll whose name is Doby. Then Doby entered the song, and came to school today. She expanded the game, and Mozart came to school today. Then it was Da Vinci and Che Guevara. These figures "came to school" because books with their names or faces were all around the room.

She would pick up a book and put it beside me and go back to her spot and shake the rattle and incorporate the new figure into the song. In this way Shakespeare came to school today, and Van Gogh, Alice in her wonderland, Frida Kahlo, Winnie-the-Pooh, Paddington Bear, Picasso, and Vermeer. She stood there with an odd look in her eye, shaking the rattle and singing.

"I like this school," I said, "with all these wonderful people attending."

But she paid me no mind. With a strangely stubborn will, she went on shaking the rattle. Then "ballet came to school." Then her twelve imaginary friends.

I delight in these precocious displays of my daughter, for they confirm the sense that she is a phenomenon of some indefinable kind.

She was still in the center of the living room, the rattle shaking less and less, as she found more people who were coming to school. Her father watched nervously. He always felt she had a magical condition. There were times he watched her as nervously as you might watch a seismograph recording unprecedented activity. Her sensitivity to unexpected impulses was a regular part of her personality. Every day she absorbed into her mythology all the people she met and all the characters in books she encountered. She became them, she took on their names.

*

My husband watched her with a mixture of wonder and nervousness that kept him on tenterhooks. Then it seemed she had run out of people who came to school that morning. She paused.

"Guess who else came to school today?" she said, with a smile that had become more mysterious.

"Who else came to school today, sweetie?" my husband and I asked with one voice, sitting on the edge of our seats.

"Death came to school today,

Death came to school today."

My husband and I looked at one another, in consternation. She was shaking her rattle, with that odd look, that sly smile on her face. She raised her hands up, and the rattle now seemed to sound from above. We looked up at the ceiling.

"The death of the world came to school today,

The end of the world came to school today…"

"Honey, dear one," I said, with a strangled note of distress in my voice, "who taught you to say that?"

"Yes, darling, who taught you that?" my husband said, standing up.

Then she held out her arms, palms facing us, commanding us to stop. We froze. It was as if she were the teacher and we the students.

"No one is going to school again,

No one is going to sch—"

We stopped her and carried her off to bed. It was the sense that she was talking prophecy that got to us. You know, out of the mouths of babes...

Two days later the flooding began in the city. Water rose suddenly, flooding the first floors. On television the politicians still denied that climate change had anything to do with it and blamed it all on terrorists and socialists—

SUDDENLY IN VENICE
THE RAVENS SING

This was found in a house in a place once called Venice. Some pages are missing.

*

—the barriers came down, and the waters of the world crowded in upon us. And above the ravens were wheeling.

Officially the city is closed to the outside world. The lagoon is swollen high. It is no longer its famous blue. It is now the color of corpses and dead animals.

We watch the lagoon invade the streets, conquering our houses. The bells are tolling for the bodies found. Our deaths are lonely. We are shut up in our houses, without electricity, or water. Nothing to eat. I watch the water rising high up the buildings.

It has been rising for years, but we did not pay attention. We have been like the frog in the story, the frog in the pot of water who was slowly boiled to death without knowing it.

Every day the city got hotter, the water rose micro-inch by micro-inch, and still we said there was no conclusive evidence of anything we should worry about. The scientists were divided. Their interpretations varied depending on who was sponsoring their research. I took no interest in these things. I had ceased watching the news, not wanting to be depressed by the negative things that helped sell newspapers and television programs. I thought the whole climate business was above my head, and I left it to the specialists.

But even I could see that the temperature in Venice wasn't right. When I walked across the piazza to see my boyfriend, pigeons dropped from the air, in midflight. I saw a woman collapse near the door of San Marco. The heat was sometimes so unbearable that I wondered if I had been transported to the Sahara Desert. I couldn't make sense of the apocalyptic paradox of things: the sluggish water rising, the heat becoming muggier. Priests expired in the midst of their sermons, and were carried out feet first to the vestibule.

Last June it snowed for a whole day. Gondoliers stared in amazement at the frozen canals. The hospitals received at least a hundred cases of pneumonia. Two days later it was boiling again, and many old women perished, and old men were seen crumpling over their walking sticks all across the city. One day, not long ago, fishes appeared belly-up in the canals and the lagoons. The fishermen's nets were crammed with fish that had been dead for some time. The odor of the lagoons became unbearable, and still no one believed that these biblical signs were in any way sinister.

Our capacity for denial is stronger than our capacity for belief. We find it easier to not face the truth. We go on living our ordinary lives while refusing to believe the overwhelming evidence that our way of life is destroying us. Prisoners of the past, we go on doing things that we know are killing us. Worse, we believe that the inevitable conclusion of all our deeds will not come to pass. We think that somehow, at the last minute, there will be a miracle, a magical solution. We possibly even hope that factors in nature we hadn't considered will somehow wipe clean the slate of our environmental crimes.

The trouble is that there were normal days followed by flashes of abnormality. There were more normal than abnormal days. So we went on believing that normality was the norm, and that anything abnormal was a minor aberration. We didn't realize that normality was an unseen equilibrium whose condition had altered. The dire results of that alteration weren't apparent to us yet.

In those normal times, we watched weddings in the square. We watched brides skipping over the rising runnels of water, their white bridal dresses hitched high.

As the months went past, fewer tourists came to the city. Solitude surrounded us. Day by day the sea levels rose. At first our politicians denied it. Then they hinted that it was all the work of terrorists. Rats grew bigger and bolder. They scuttled around in daylight and didn't run away when people appeared. It was as if they had finally claimed possession of the city. But they were not the real menace. The real menace were the politicians smoothly denying there was anything to fear. But we were the worst menace of all. The way we kept trying to live normally.

Our addiction to normality might be our most pernicious quality. In the mornings, when I wake, I mutter a few lines my mother taught me. I bathe, have a coffee, and walk to the office. I work as if it were the only thing in the world that mattered. In the evening I walk home. On the way to work, I always pass the cafes in the square. I watch the waiters laying out the tables. No one is coming, but they lay out the tables as if a horde of tourists might descend on them within the hour.

I read in the newspapers that yet again the American government has refused to take part in any climate change conferences and has declared in an official statement that climate change is a myth. I read also that all across America cities are sinking beneath the rising sea. In many cities people are having to move their possessions to higher ground. They are living in tents and hastily constructed shacks. Apparently, America is in trauma. People can't seem to believe that their normality has been so radically altered. The Italian papers say there's no rioting, no protesting – just a sullen mood everywhere, like a people unwilling to wake from a long dream of certainty.

There are news stories from other lands. The facts are too strange to relate. Sometimes it seems as if newspapers are trying to outdo each other in the strange things they report. Weirdness has become universal reality.

But each day, as I walk to work, there is a waiter I always wish to catch a glimpse of when I pass the cafes. He is not tall, like the man of the average female fantasy, and he is not thin, and his eyes are not blue. He is slight of build, and quiet, and he notices things. I saw him talking to a stray cat once. Then on another day I saw him feeding the cat a bowl of milk. Such quiet sympathy is rare in these times, when we're all pulling up the drawbridges of our lives—

THE STATE DEPARTMENT DENIES

This came from a piece of metal which puzzled us for a long time, till we wondered if it coded some sort of information. When we unlocked it we found numerous photographs of a family and a city. There were images of cats and flooded streets and processions. The images began happy, but gradually turned grim. There were scraps of love letters. There was the beginning of a poem, some drawings of a child, then this. All signs show that this note was not meant to be discovered, but was written as a secret confessional. We surmised that it was written by an official of the government who clearly had access to inside information.

*

The State Department put out its official statement today about the myth of climate change. The president himself, who is temperamentally opposed to the idea of climate change, gave the statement – with significant modifications – from the Oval Office. It was repeated by the news media. He especially wanted to make this statement to kill off the wild speculation that has been driving people into frenzies of despair. He made it clear that the fluctuations of nature, the persistent flooding, the accelerated number of typhoons that blast our shores, and the forest fires that destroyed half of California are all natural acts and in no way amount to anything out of the ordinary. They've been going on for years. Strange occurrences do not suggest Armageddon.

There was a research project set up in the department to study bizarre events over the years. It turns out that every year has had its share of strange occurrences, and this is true going back a hundred years. It seems that we exaggerate the significance of the strange occurrences of our own times. We think them unique. The report was a much-needed corrective to the doom-mongering that has become fashionable. Compared to past eras abundant with terrible events, our times are underperforming in the field of disasters. Just think of Vesuvius erupting, of Pompeii, of forest fires that raged for weeks, of the earlier ages of global warming that set the scene for *Homo sapiens* to appear on the world stage. Think of the climactic conditions that wiped out the woolly mammoths.

It is not fashionable for scientists to say this now, or they would be crucified by the public, but in their private reports they maintain that fluctuations in weather conditions, the fires and storms, have been part of the history of the earth for millennia. When human beings had religion they blamed natural catastrophes on the wrath of God or the gods. Now they blame governments and corporations. We are the new gods. And we have decreed that there is no global warming.

And even if there is, so what? We are planning our relocation to Mars. There, we'll start again – with the chosen few. Why do people think that the earth is irreplaceable?

It is merely a coincidence that of the million planets in the universe this is the only one stable enough to be a home for life. But that stability was always fragile. Humanity was always going to evolve, and evolution means destruction. It is the law of evolution itself. We always kick the ladder from beneath us. That is the way we go forward.

Pollution is the by-product of evolution, the price we paid for civilization. Those who wish we had evolved differently not only deny history but also deny the tremendous benefits they have enjoyed. I can't stand those teenage doomsayers who live in the luxury of the West, and all that this implies in the destruction of other cultures, the vast undocumented crimes of Western civilization. Do they now want, in the last moment, to somehow be absolved of history and turn back the clock?

But what if the doomsayers are right? What if the president is leading us into the end of time itself? What if we are fiddling while the world burns? And the world is burning burning burning. It's burning in the Amazon, burning in Australia, burning all over the United States. Cathedrals are burning and monks are setting themselves on fire and the ice caps are evaporating and the cities are aflame and there are heat waves in places where there should be snow.

What are we doing supporting a president who may be leading us to the death of all things? What kind of a job is this that obliges me to obey what is going to destroy us all? Are there no limits to duty? Deep down I do not believe this program of denial, but I am well paid, am one of the best at what I do, and here I am using my skills not only to tell what I think is a lie but to collude in the greatest lie of all, the terminal lie, the doomsday lie, the lie to end all lies.

For I can see with my own eyes that all is not well in the world. I was taking my daughter to nursery yesterday when an iguana fell from the sky right at my feet. My daughter, who is five, and still sees everything with a touch of wonder, said:

"Daddy, why are iguanas falling from the sky?"

What was I to say? Was I to give her the president's lie, that it is nothing unusual, that it happens all the time? I tried silence, hoping her mind would find something else to interest her. But I had forgotten the persistence of a five-year-old.

"Why, Daddy, why are iguanas falling from the sky? One fell just now. Look at it. But why…"

"It happens from time to time, sweetie," I said.

"Is it God who is throwing them down? Is God angry with iguanas, Daddy?"

"No," I said, "God is not angry with iguanas."

"Is God angry with us?"

This stopped me in my tracks. It hit me in my solar plexus, winding me, like an unexpected Houdini punch. The kind that kills you two days later.

"What was that, sweetie?"

"Why is God angry with us?"

"I don't think God is."

"What have we done to make him angry?"

"Why do you say that, sweetie?"

She had pulled her little hand out of mine and stood

there looking up at the sky. Then she screwed her face into a puzzled frown.

"Because of the way he is throwing down the iguanas."

I stood there at a loss. For the first time, I felt trapped in a lie that I had been spinning for the sake of raising this very same person who was exposing it with her innocent questions.

"It's not God who is throwing them down."

"Then who is?"

I was silent again.

"And why are there so many people without homes, Daddy? Why do they all sleep in the streets?"

"Because their homes have gone under the sea," I said, without thinking, partly out of exasperation at my own powerlessness.

"But why did the sea rise so high?"

"It's hard to explain."

"Are we all going under the sea, Daddy?"

For the first time I became aware of the intelligence of my own daughter. She seemed to be speaking with a hidden knowledge, and she was looking at me as if I knew something but wasn't sharing. Maybe it was just the natural skepticism of children.

"Of course we're not all going under the sea!" I said, almost explosively.

She caught her breath. Then she gave me a disapproving look.

"Where did you get that funny idea?" I asked, as soothingly as I could.

"The other kids at school."

"Pay them no attention. They don't know anything."

"And do you, Daddy?"

I broke out in something of a sweat as another iguana landed at our feet. She didn't flinch this time, just went on staring at me.

That's when it happened.

That's when I suddenly burst out crying and didn't know why and couldn't seem to stop.

I was crouching low now, down to her level, sobbing my eyes out. People were watching us. That made it worse.

"Now, now," my daughter said, patting my back, touching my face. "Don't worry, Daddy. We're all going under the sea. We'll just have to learn to live like fishes."

THOSE DEEP MINES

Fragments found in what was Africa. This was a scrap from the faded pages of a magazine.

*

The only time I remember being happy was when I was coming out of the mines. I'd be covered in bauxite dust, my eyes rimmed with it. We went down in our ordinary clothes and canvas shoes. They would drill and the powdery stuff would be all that we would breathe. Later, when I would blow my nose, it was blood that came out.

I thought it was all normal, and I was making money to feed my family. No one ever told me there was another way.

I always wanted to go to school, but my mother died when I was young and my father who loved her so much did not last long after she went. We had no one to look after us, and soon all seven of us found ourselves in the streets.

Our relatives didn't want to know us. Some of them tried to look after us, but they had problems of their own. Then slowly my brothers scattered, and my sister became pregnant by some man she worked for, and I never saw her again.

One day a man asked if I wanted easy money, and I said yes. Then he got me to climb the back of a fairly crowded truck. Then he took us to this place far out of the city.

They put us in this shaft. Before I knew it we were going down into the earth. On that first day I thought I would die. I thought I was going down into hell.

All the others with me were also going down for the first time. I don't know where they found them. They all looked pale. Stray dog humans who had no homes and no families. If they died no one would notice, no one would care.

We were mine-fodder. I remember the day, not long after I started, when the mine collapsed while we were inside. They didn't come to rescue us. All the rocks and earth collapsed over us, and we had only the dangerous red dust to breathe. The few of us who were alive had to dig our way out. It took almost a whole day. When we came out into the light, they fined us and then had us jailed for the collapse of the mines. We were in jail when we heard about the collapse of four other mines.

Then we heard about the earthquakes in the northern provinces. We heard tales of the earth splitting open and whole villages falling through the gaps. We heard of the land shifting and forests disappearing and the waves rushing over the cities and burying the tractors and the offices and the flowers. We heard of tornadoes that flung houses into the air. Cities swirled in the storm, rising to the sky and scattering before crashing back down to earth. We heard of trees upside down in the wind and of the people panicking and the churches smashed by the fist of hurricanes.

Then we heard that the world we knew was gone. It had all vanished into the white hole of the storm, and no one knew where it went. It seemed that those of us who were trapped down in the mines and rotting in prison were the only ones saved. The storms blew the roof off the prison, and for a moment the sky revealed to us our limitless freedom. Then we went out into a world in which there were only stones—

AND THE GODS DEPARTED

This fragment was found wedged beneath a giant rock, a page from an unidentified book.

*

We were singing on the way to the shrine in the baobab forest. The spirits were taller than the trees. A blue mist hung from the iroko leaves. We heard the chattering voices of the spirits. They buzzed from below, as if speaking from the earth. But it is a trick they have, of throwing their voices, of making it take on the sound of leaves or lizards, just to confuse those who are not supposed to come into the forest.

We stopped singing as we entered the forest. We had been singing of our grief. The world had gone upside down and inside out. Nothing made sense anymore. We had been charged by the elders and the grief-stricken people to ask the oracle what was going on in the world.

The rivers had gone mad. The sky no longer behaved like a sky. The rivers were boiling, but the sky sent down white powder. What did it all mean? Sometimes it was very cold and ice appeared on the ground. Then the next day it would be so hot that every living thing would burn, and human beings would drop to the ground, and birds would crash into walls as if they could not see. The world was not normal anymore. Everywhere people in churches and mosques prayed and sang. But things were getting worse.

Then the elders decreed that we should go back to the old gods and the shrines and the ancestors and find out what they had to tell us. They chose me to be one of the supplicants. I am one whose head has been shaven by the terrible things of life. My eyes have been peeled by pain and trouble. I am a penitent at the feet of tragedy.

I was surprised when they chose me to lead the procession. As we walked into the depths of the forest, I beat a gong through the night to drive away unwanted spirits. We went deep into sacred terrain, to where the old gods still dwell. No one has been there since the days of the shrines, which are now lost and tangled in mangrove roots, embedded in the thick forest.

We went in there fearing that the old gods and spirits were angry with us for having abandoned them all these decades. No one could remember the last time we had gone to the shrine. No one could remember where the shrine was. We only found it again through clues in children's songs and half-forgotten stories pieced together from our memories.

In this way we made our way back to the abandoned shrine. The path was overgrown with vines. We had to cut out the way anew. We encountered large turtles. The mangrove swamp had widened. There were wild red flowers among the exposed roots. They looked like blood scattered everywhere.

After much hacking at vines and climbers, after finding the old trail, after baulking at fleshlike flowers and smooth-skinned mottled pythons that were clearly descendants of the pythons of the old shrines, after making our way through the marsh, we found that the old shrine was protected and pristine. It was as if the priests of the old gods had been coming here, in secret, to clean their sacred spaces. But this had not been so. We beheld the freshness of the shrine with a mixture of wonder and horror.

All at once the herbalists who were with us rushed to the preserved shrine and fell in prostration before the bronze images of Ogun and Eshu, the father god and the trickster god. The herbalists and priests began jabbering at once. We stood back and watched this weird transformation. The herbalists became different people, their voices much deeper. Their faces wore distracted smiles.

While we were still recovering from the shock of finding

the place intact, the shrine began to speak. The shrine spoke through the herbalists. We watched them contort and howl, as if possessed by unbearable agony. At first we feared they had been struck by snakes or scorpions or bitten by vicious insects. They began to thrash on the floor, their faces twisted. Then one of them began to drool and to shout out words that no one had heard before. We were transfixed.

Then my body received the communication. I don't know how. I received it. The earth was howling through these herbalists. Then the howl of the earth seized me. I flung myself against a tree and began to scream as if someone had plugged an electric cable into my intimate parts. Then just as suddenly, the pain stopped. A moment of calm came over me. It seemed like the calm of death.

Then I saw the gods. They were leaving, in a procession. They did not look back. They took everything with them, the secrets of the land, the icons of the ancestors, the threads and beads and links to the spirit world. They took it all as they left our realm.

Then I knew that the end had come. I wanted to join them, but I was too much of this world. If there was ever a moment I wished myself dead, that was it. For now that they were going, we would be marooned here, useless witnesses of a world about to pass away.

All we could do was watch them leave. They left without any farewell gesture. It was as if they knew that among our many gifts as human beings was a genius for obliterating the future—

A VISION ONCE I SAW

Found half-stuffed in a bottle in the forests of Peru.

*

We came here because we wanted a vision that would surpass the negativity of the daily news. Every day brought some new horror.

We came out to Peru, to see the shaman a friend had recommended. We were going to take part in a rite which culminated in the ayahuasca ceremony.

Daily life had become weird. Everyone we knew was sinking into drink and despair. Many of my mates took their own lives. They checked out before life checked out on them. It was a pre-emptive strike against death. There was just too much death around. We wanted to make a pitch for life.

The shaman was a small man with yellow-green eyes. As if he distrusted words, he didn't speak much. Would that I could write this with silence. He made us sit in a circle and took us through a ceremony that we were meant to keep secret. Then we each drank the potion, its bitterness mitigated by a cube of sugar. I lay on a large feather cushion, and at first nothing happened. Then the fabric of time and space bent, and reality altered, and I found myself on a boat on the vast sea.

It was the last boat in the world. It had golden, red and orange sails. The sea was tinged with purple and green. The sky, bent over the curvature of the world, had a reddish haze. The boat had three levels. On one level were the last children left in the world, nine boys and nine girls. They were kept apart in separate compartments so they wouldn't meet and have any intercourse. They had to be kept pure. They were the last children left in a world that had gone wrong.

On a deeper level of the boat were all the animal species left in the world, two of each. It somehow did not seem possible that all the birds and beasts fitted into that space. And in the deepest level of the boat, at the very bottom, was something strange. It was something like a sound, or a light, an energy. It was both infinite and small. It was the secret force of the whole world. But I did not know what it was or who had put it there.

The boat was drawn by swans. The swans brought the boat through storms with a calm that was almost supernatural. At the side of the boat, helping the swans at their tasks, were eight octopuses.

On the third day of the boat's journey to the place where we'd all be saved, the children started making love to one another. This was a bit alarming, as they were not supposed to do that. They were meant to arrive at the place where we'd be saved, pristine and innocent. The sea was now purple, but the sky was a color I had never seen before. I had no idea where we were going or what it was we were fleeing. All I knew then was that perhaps time was no more.

It came to me that disease and fire and the rising sea, despair and atmospheric poisons, had overwhelmed the earth. History was over. The time of narrative was gone. All that was left were the frail dreams that floated in solitude upon the sea.

"And at the end of the world," a girl in the boat was saying, as if she were making up a new story, "peace will return."

Then the voice drifted away upon the wind.

*

These were some of the stories we found. In a way, the girl in the last fragment was right. Peace had returned to the planet. It was the most beautiful of the planets that we saw in our journeys across the galaxies. It was certainly the only one that showed rich evidence of life.

We collected many artifacts and scraps of machines. Humans seemed to have used plastic, glass, and metal in most of their daily activities. From all the evidence we have, they seem to have worshipped *things*. They did not seem capable of great ideas. They seem to have been oddly limited in their philosophy. Their images were of themselves. They saw everything only through themselves.

Unlike older civilizations we encountered, civilizations that died out hundreds of thousands of years ago, this one showed no especially exalted conception of the universe. The people had no sense of the almost infinite possibility of it all. They seemed a rather parochial and tribal species, bedeviled by ideas of race and gender. Not for a single moment during their relatively short history did they see themselves as part of a universal order. This sense of cosmic nobility eluded them.

It is perhaps this inability to rise above their limited perception of themselves, and a passionate identification with what was smallest in themselves, that explains why they could not transcend the doom that they saw approaching them. It was a doom which they contributed to every day, and which they were unable to alter.

Perhaps a people's capacity for change is only as great as their understanding of their spiritual patrimony. They thought themselves dust, and to dust they returned.

It gives one a pang of inexpressible sadness to know that this magical planet was once home to the glory that was their lives.

*

On this 5xxxxx eon of progress, we leave the earth behind and resume our mapping of planets that once bore witness to the magnificence of being.

TIGER WORK

Prowls the edges
Dwindling in cages
Into legend falling
From collective memory fading.
Hunted every hour
For its eyes, its stripes, its power
When it vanishes we will follow.
Its absence will make us hollow.
It lives in language, lives in lore.
That death begins in thought is a kind of law.

And if it exists no longer
Would this make weak or stronger
Our spiritual reach,
Our poetry and speech?
It prowls dream and song
And links us to earth and sun
And every day we grow smaller
With the death of a single one.
The loss of the fly
Is as great as that of the tiger
And the death of the last bug
As tragic as the death of the Niger.

We need some ferocity
To protect our humanity
Need mystery and presence
To project force and the sense
Of justice. Our rights
Depend on our mental fights.
We need spirit power
In the streets and tower
Need it in the totem and high place
As guardian spirit of the human race
Need it in the struggles of the street
Where climate denial and end of time meet.
What else can mesmerize
Like the beauty of its eyes?

It belongs to a higher order
Composed of fire, mystery, dreams,
Conjunction of power and radiance
Something prophetic it seems
A compacted state of being
Something we'll never accomplish
Never get to, much as we would wish.
An alternative route of evolution
Form and sign of a divine solution.

Something about it is too much for us
Like simple addition next to calculus
Stuns us with the limitation of our form
And our messy everyday norm.

Tells us we can be more.
Leap into better destinies than before.
Primed for great battles ahead
Between those who want us dead
And those who want to lift
The human song to its highest gift.

If we are to survive
Fighting spirit must we revive
If we as a race will thrive
Tiger spirit must we keep alive.

THE HOUSE BELOW

The mother and her three sons lived in a small flat in a two-story building. There was a marsh in front of their house, where mosquitoes bred. Their house was on a little street off the main road. It used to be a dirt track, but cars and lorries now made it usable.

There were workshops along the street where the bodyworks of the big yellow buses of Lagos were built. In the mornings sparks flew from welding equipment. The mechanics, as they were called, never wore any face guards.

There was an abattoir towards the middle of the street. Next to it was a school. The school had no doors or windows. Its walls were raw unplastered cement bricks. Goats that were to be slaughtered were tethered in the school building after class hours. The goats never liked being tethered there. They seemed terrified and reared and tugged at the ropes whenever anyone came near them. It was as if they sensed the imminence of their deaths. The children went to school in a place haunted by dead animals.

The mother and her sons lived in the house opposite the school. The building was not as old as it looked. The landlord also owned the house next door, a long bungalow crammed with tenants who had large families. Sometimes as many as seven people lived in one room.

The mother rented a two-room flat on the ground floor of the main house. There was another family at the back, but she didn't see them often. The rooms were small. She made the first into a living room and the second into a bedroom. These rooms held all the contents of a life that spanned two continents. She slept in the inner room, while her sons slept on the sofa and on mats on the floor of the outer room.

The house had been built as part of the scramble for land that happened as the city expanded. Without original permits, and with papers often put together after some bribe to the right people in the department of land development, landlords built houses wherever they found space. There was little town planning back then. That came later. Roads grew from paths that were once tracks that led to hamlets and isolated communities in the bush. The city expanded and encompassed the communities. The tracks used by cows and goats became paths and then roads. They had never been tarred and became hard and dusty in the dry season and turned to mud when it rained.

The houses were haphazardly built. Some would be at an angle to the road. Then others would be set in complete contradiction to those. The angles were all wrong but no one cared. A comprehensive survey of the land had never been done, and streets sprang up because someone stuck a name on a plank of wood. That sign became the street's name. Sometimes streets acquired their names through rumor or through proximity to some factory or a notable place in the neighborhood, which could be a celebrated buka or a local market.

When the mother moved into the house, it was a fine-looking building. It was mustard-colored and four-square in the bright sunlight. Within a year, its paint had faded to a mouse gray color, the color of dirt and mud and finger stains. The doors were blue and the roof was of solid zinc. It was the first building you saw from the bus stop across the marshland.

To deter thieves, it had a gray wall round its perimeter. All the windows had metal grilles with locks so they couldn't be opened from the outside. The wall had barbed wire running along its top, and from within it looked as if you were not in your house but inside a small prison.

By the second year the color of the doors had faded and the toilet had become clogged. But the strangest thing of all, which no one noticed for a long time, was that when they went out of the house they found the world aslant, out of kilter. For a long time the family had the certainty that the land had been wrenched from its original orientation. They sensed it every day when they went out, whether it was to work or school. It was only when they came back home that the world made sense again.

The family were kept close by the skewing of the world, the broken axis of things. They drew close together and told one another stories. They reinforced themselves with a mythology of the family created every day. It meant little to them that they lived on the edge of desperation. The mother worked hard at maintaining her dignity against the outrages of an undignified world. These things only strengthened their mythology, only deepened the intensity of their closeness.

Outside the house, the world was disintegrating. No one seemed to notice. More houses were built in the mind-boggling disorder of the area. Some people built houses that projected right into the street.

Some built their houses at street corners, forcing people to navigate their way round the obstacle of their property. Foundations were sunk into the ground and metal poles stuck up out of the earth and concrete mixers whirled outside the yard. And before you knew it a two-story building sprang up, waiting to be weighed down with families burdened with poverty.

Front rooms became beer parlors or carpenters' sheds or barber shops. Neon-lit signboards appeared advertising some new establishment. Sometimes it was a record shop. Apala music or the vibrations of Afrobeat would pound in the air along with the dust that rose from the scooters and the yellow taxis that struggled along the impromptu streets.

Meanwhile in the nation outside there were coups followed by coups. The daily newspapers coughed up the bile of corruption, the daily outrages to the public coffers. Vast sums went missing. Politicians were accused of kickbacks. Military governors awarded themselves lucrative contracts for roads that would never be built. And the children went to school in unfinished buildings, with half-erected walls through which they could see the horrified goats tethered and waiting to be slaughtered.

The mother lived in all of this with great dignity. She sustained the family with the salt of proverbs and the magic of stories. She had dreams in which her children, one by one, in their different spheres, triumphed in the world. The bad water and the ruined sewers affected her health but she kept her ailing condition to herself. To her children she showed not only remarkable courage but also unfailing good humor. She had a story for everything and there was not anything good or bad that she could not transfigure with a tale.

The world was tilting. The world was sinking. The city throbbed with energy and rage. People argued everywhere. The buses pumped out clouds of poisonous fumes. The factories darkened the skyline with their murky emissions. Roadside traders chanted their wares. Children returned from school, faces pasted with dust and smoke, clothes dirty with fumes coagulating in the air.

Sometimes in the evenings there were spectacular parties. Whole streets were taken over for weddings or funeral celebrations. Once there was a wedding party that went on for three days. None of the neighbors were consulted. The street was laid out with tables and chairs. Women came in lace wrappers and gorgeous head ties, men in sokotos and agbadas. Most families came in matching outfits. There were interminably long speeches. A band played on an improvised stand. Well into the night their voices rang over the houses and the fume-covered banana plants and the dusty palm trees. At these parties there was always dancing and laughter and quarrels and fights. The reconciliations were as dramatic as the altercations that caused the fighting.

The world rested on nothing and they weighed it down with all that passion, all that disorder. The earth was unstable too but no one knew. No one had consulted her. No one had spoken to her, asked her permission, or investigated her disposition. Everything was laid on her – vast skyscrapers, thundering lorries, gigantic drilling machines. All night the road roared with vehicles. It never stopped. From the house, the road and the world could be heard as through an infinite megaphone. When they didn't hear it with their ears, they felt it through the vibration of things.

Then one day the mother stepped out of the house and found that the door was not at the right level. She had to step higher to go out. She had to duck her head acutely so as not to crack it against the upper part of the jamb. On another day the eldest son coming back home from work couldn't quite find the house. He had to look harder than before. Then with an extraordinary effort of will he brought it back into being, as if pulling it up from oblivion.

That same son went away for a long time and when he came back confirmed for himself that all things tend to shrink in memory. Everything seemed smaller on his return. The school building seemed sadder and smaller, the goats seemed scrawnier, and the bungalow behind their house seemed like an enlarged matchbox. Their house was unrecognizable. It was hotter inside. Fabulous ingenuity was now conscripted for the moving of bowels. There were so many new houses in the area that the street had become a big obstacle course.

The heat made everything worse. Tempers flared and policemen took to flogging cars and motorcyclists. In compounds and rooms voices were raised to an unnatural pitch. The economy staggered along and elections were rigged and every few years the military came back in a coup.

The house that they lived in grew unbearably hot at night. Even the ceiling fan did not make sleep easier. The mother grew thinner, worked harder, helped her relations, and one by one her children flew the nest.

On the day the eldest left, she was to drive him to the airport. He looked back at the house with tears of fondness. It was the house in which he had been nourished with his mother's love and stories. He had been close to his brothers. The rooms were small but the stories they shared made them large. Sometimes they would tell one another stories till late into the night. They told stories while the family upstairs quarreled so implacably that they added to the weight of the house. They told stories through coups and the return to democracy, through the sapping of the nation's resources and through the constant failures of electricity.

The eldest son stood there and looked at the house as if for the first time. It was then he noticed something that had evaded him all along. But what he noticed could not be true. It must have been an illusion produced by the strong emotion of leaving.

He noticed not only that the house was smaller but also that it was disappearing into the earth. The top floor was much lower than it had been years ago. He was about to share this discovery with his mother when she looked at her watch.

"It's a long journey, you know," she said. "And traffic will be terrible."

They set off immediately and he forgot all about the sinking condition of the house. He traveled to France and Greece and to the United States of America. Then he settled in England, where he devoted himself to the study of meaning.

The house kept quiet about its condition. This was not always the case. Sometimes the house spoke but no one listened. The landlord, increasingly certain that the house was in one of the prime locations of the city, doubled the rent. For the first time the mother began to think of leaving.

The house spoke to the tenants but they were too terrified to hear. The house spoke to the landlord but he was too proud and greedy to think that the house even had a right to speak for itself. So the house sank into its own silence and communed with the earth.

One day a daughter of the tenant who lived in the back rooms tried to leave the house to go to school, but found that she could not leave. The door would not open. Her parents thought she was looking for an excuse not to go to school and with a great effort they got the door open. They could not understand what had happened.

That night the mother had a dream that the house was becoming a tomb and that she was living not in a house but in a pharaonic coffin. She had been reading a book about ancient Egypt, which spoke of the coffins not as places of death, but as the beginnings of the house of eternity. The dream had so troubled the mother that she decided the time really had come for her to leave.

A month later she and her remaining children hired a lorry. They had great trouble bringing out the bed and the center table and the sofa. The door had somehow become too small for them. But eventually everything was out and they were set to leave. The mother took one last look at the house, just as her eldest son had done some time ago, and what she saw amazed her.

The house now seemed to be only the top floor. That was all that was visible. It did not seem possible to her that she had been living in a house that had been vanishing all this time. How is it that none of them had seen it? Was it the tyranny of daily perception, or had the house somehow conspired to envelop them in its fantasy?

The mother was on the verge of saying something about it to her sons but the lorry driver had a fit of Lagosian impatience and wanted to be off so he could get in a few more jobs before the day was over. The mother said nothing. But she retained in her mind the image of the shrunken house that had once been their home.

*

The mother moved onto her own land, on which she built a house. She no longer thought about the house that had been left behind. But the house thought of her. The house missed her stories. She had thought she was telling stories to her children and receiving their stories in turn. But they had all been sharing their stories with the house. That was how the house had managed to delay its disappearance into the earth. All those stories had kept it buoyant, made it float, as it were, to the rhythms of other lands, other homes, other destinies.

When the mother left, the landlord rented her rooms to a large family of ten. They brought with them squabbles and noise. They had to crawl in through the gap at the top of the front door, which had been removed altogether. When they went out for the day, they had to crawl back through the tight space. They brought the weight of their troubles and their hunger. The young children cried all night in the unrelieved heat.

Then came the season of politicians who excelled in the art of taking without giving. They didn't care very much about the earth or the fumes or the lungs of the people or the loss of the forests or the terror of the goats or the unfinished school building where the children carried on their incomplete education.

And the house, starved of stories, deprived of fine and far-fetched dreams, lost its levity and its humor.

Then one day, just before the big rains that swept in from the east, the house lost the will to go on existing, lost the will to maintain its coherence. The tenants went on living there, for years and years to come. They went on living there even when the house had sunk so completely into the earth that only the roof was visible.

The landlord provided ladders and ropes for the tenants who now lived below the earth. This way they could get out when they went to work or school. He was even kind enough to provide them with light extensions and free candles when the electricity failed, hour after hour, all through the night and through most of the day.

The family lived below the ground like moles. Out of their windows they saw only the earth. Sometimes water seeped up into the living room. The landlord showed his understanding by lowering the rent for the duration of the seepage. The family of ten lived down there enclosed all around by the dark and the heat. Sometimes, huddled in their silence, in the blaze of their eyes as they stared with anxiety at one another, they heard scattered fragments of all the stories that the house had stored and played back to itself in the twilight of its existence.

Then one day the house disappeared and no one knew that it had ever been there.

SPAWN

By-product of the devil's fuel.
Adapted itself to our deeds
Our carrying, our containers,
Our wrapping, our
Packaging. Has
Come from nature
But is itself unnatural.
Is undegradable.
Forever lingering.
Sticks in the guts
Of fishes and dolphins.
Will last a thousand years
And be there when
We have all gone to dust.

What is this thing
That we have made
So essential?
A film between
Us and the world.
Landfills are crammed
With its incarnations.
Curse of modern living.
They say now that
Its microfibers can
Be found
In our blood, in
Our cells.

Slowly we have
Become
Part human, part
Plastic.

FROM A SACRED PLACE

We say that there is a climate emergency. But it is truer to say that there is a humanity emergency. The climate crisis is caused by us human beings, because we have forgotten the intimate relationship we have with nature. We treat nature like a resource, a thing to use without end, for profit and for our ascendancy. In this way we treat nature like an enemy.

But when we contemplate the roots of the climate crisis we are led to the fact that the earliest cases of the abuse of nature coincided with imperialism, with the conquistadors, with the quest for other places to plunder. In short, the abuse of nature began with our abuse of our fellow human beings. Then the plunder of nature was exacerbated by colonial and capitalist expansion and the needs of what we call civilization.

The climate crisis is not really about the climate. It's about us.

The only possible solution is to re-sacralize our fellow human beings, and to re-sacralize nature. Since we stripped the divine from our fellow human beings we made it easier to dehumanize them. And when we tore the divine from nature we made it easier to treat her so outrageously.

The climate crisis cannot be solved in isolation. It is a problem for the whole of the human race. It seems that the future for us requires re-engaging all of humanity, and understanding that we are all on the same ship, and that we can only solve this crisis together.

We need a new vision of the human. Not one based on division and perceived exceptionalism but one based on the truth that we are inescapably part of one another.

The only way to heal the climate crisis is to heal ourselves.

We are the crisis, the emergency, and the catastrophe. And there will be no permanent solution to environmental disasters till we heal the disaster that is our divisive and selfish thinking.

In Sophocles's *Oedipus Rex*, the story is told of a land cursed with pestilence and famine. People send to the oracle to find the cause. The king intends to punish whoever is responsible. In the end, it turns out that the king himself is the guilty one. That's how it is with us. We want to find the causes of environmental catastrophe. We point fingers and allocate blame. But, in the end, it turns out that we are the guilty ones. Our whole way of life is the greatest threat to our survival. We are daily, indirectly, committing the suicide of the human race.

But it is not just in our emissions, our poisoning of the air, our polluting of the seas. It is really in why we do it. We do it for industry, for electricity, for commerce. These are the reasons why the big nations are finally unable to implement the scale of change needed to pull us back from the brink of the apocalypse.

No country wants to lose its advantages. None wants to lose its position. The politicians know that most of their citizens will vote them out if living standards fall below an acceptable level. That is why leaders say one thing and do another.

We are in a different kind of cold war now. We are in a resources war. We are in an economic war. No one in the West wants to scale down their lifestyle. It is this same greed that led to conquests and colonies, the same need that fueled the Industrial Revolution and the economic transformation of Europe and America, Russia and China.

The quest for power and resources means we pollute, we devastate, we rape the earth. Energy drives our economies, the very same energy that is polluting our world.

A thread runs from that early restless quest for power and resources to our contemporary environmental crisis.

A huge healing is called for. A new vision of the human future is needed. It ought to be one that respects nature and other human beings, one that finds a manageable way to be a civilization.

THE SONGBIRD'S SILENCE

(a story for children)

Once upon a time, not that long ago, the forest was full of noises. You could hear the birds sing, or the faraway growl of a wolf, or the call of cats, or the constant trilling of insects. The forest was a busy place at night because all the creatures were claiming their space. They were saying, with the noises they made, that this was their home.

Then human beings began to capture the creatures of the forest. Some liked to have the butterflies as friends. Some wanted the tigers as pets. But the creature they wanted most was the songbird. It was not the most beautiful bird in the world but it had the most enchanting song. Its song was so wonderful that people wanted the songbird in their house so they could live always with the strange and charming music it made. Soon everybody wanted one.

There was once a little boy who lived near the forest. His name was Duba. He used to love going to sleep at night and listening to the many mysterious noises of the forest. As he went to sleep at night he would imagine all the things the animals were doing. It seemed to him that as he was going to sleep they were waking up. He imagined the monkeys chattering and telling one another stories. He imagined the birds in long singing competitions. And he imagined the wild dogs growling in their nightly attempts to talk to the moon. He loved these imaginings of his and they helped him sleep nicely at night.

Then one day it was Duba's birthday and as a present his father and mother gave him a songbird. It came in a big cage. Duba was very happy with his present. He had never had a pet before and never come that close to a bird before either. And it was such a special thing to listen to the songbird's melodies in the morning and at night. He was very grateful to his mother and father for giving him such a wonderful present. He grew very attached to the bird and wanted to be with it all the time. He was only really happy when the bird was singing.

Duba was so fascinated by the bird's songs that he wanted to know what it was singing about and why its singing was so sweet. Sometimes when the songbird sang Duba would be so moved that he would begin crying. The beauty of the song was so haunting that Duba took to asking everyone if they knew what the bird was singing about. His mother and father couldn't tell him. None of the elders could tell him either. Then one day Duba met a wise old man near the forest.

"O wise man," he said, "do you know why the songbird's song is so sweet? What is it saying?"

"Why are you asking me?" the wise man asked.

"Because everyone says you are a wise man."

"I think the songbird is wiser than me."

"Why do you say that?"

"Because it is singing a song that has caused you to ask many questions, and yet you do not know what it is singing about."

"So how can I find out why its song is so sweet or what it is saying?"

"I think you should ask the songbird itself."

"Ask the songbird? How? I don't speak its language. I won't understand what it says."

"How do you know?"

"Because I have tried."

"Maybe you should ask the question in a different way."

"How?"

"You will know when the time comes."

"I hope so."

"And you should listen in a different way too."

"How should I do that?"

"You should listen with more than your ears."

"More than my ears? What else should I listen with then?"

"Perhaps," said the wise man, "you should listen with your heart."

Duba was so taken with this conversation with the old man that when he got home he forgot to listen to the bird's song. He was thinking about how he could ask the question differently and how he could listen with his heart. That night he didn't sleep very well and he didn't know why. In fact, he slept very badly. He tossed and turned all night. He was aware that something was missing. Something that made his sleep lovely was gone. Then just before dawn he fell asleep. And in his sleep he had a dream. In his dream the songbird spoke to him.

"Do you want to know why my song is so sweet?"

"Yes."

"Do you also want to know what I keep saying in my songs?"

"Yes. I have been asking everyone those questions. No one could give me an answer."

"I was the only one who could give you an answer. But you had to ask the right question. And you had to listen with your heart."

"Did I ask you the right question?"

"Yes, you did."

"But how?"

"You asked it with your soul. You asked it from the part of you that really cared."

"What are the answers?"

"Have you noticed something about the world?"

"No. What should I have noticed?"

"Did you notice that something is missing?"

"Yes. But I don't know what it is."

"No one does."

"What is it?"

"The forest is silent."

"Is it? Why?"

"Because people have been treating the animals and birds badly."

"Have they?"

"Yes. Take me, for example. Do you think I am happy?"

"You must be. Your songs are so beautiful."

"My songs are beautiful because I am unhappy. My songs are trying to tell you the terrible things you are doing to the forest, to the bears, the pangolins, the iguanas, the beautiful birds, the tigers. Because you are not protecting them the forest is silent."

"Really?"

"Yes. The forest is dying."

"What can I do?"

"Listen with your heart."

"I like having you as a pet."

"I know. But I don't like being a pet. I am made to be free. You say my song is beautiful in your cage. But you should hear me sing when I am free."

"What is it like?"

"It is as if all of nature is singing, the sea, the sky, the trees, and all the majestic creatures. It is as if God is singing through me. My song when I am free is a million times richer than my song in a cage. The only song I sing in a cage is the song of tears, the song of the silent forest."

"I am so sorry."

"If you are really sorry you would do something for me."

"What is that?"

"Wake up."

Duba immediately awoke. It was still dark. He listened carefully. It was true. The forest was silent. He didn't hear the wolf cough, or the trilling of insects. He hurried to the cage. The songbird was silent. Nothing he did would make the songbird sing. Then he understood why the songbird was no longer singing.

He went and woke up his mother and father. They were surprised to see him.

"Mum and Dad," said the boy, "we have done the songbird a terrible wrong. We have taken it from the forest, its home, and now it will not sing. Because of the songbird the forest is silent. Have you not noticed?"

His mother and father listened.

"You are right," they said. "The forest is silent. How is it we never noticed?"

"We have to help the forest live again," said the boy. "First we must return the songbird to its home, but carefully. Then we have to protect the creatures of the forest, or one day we too will fall silent."

"But how do you know these things?" asked the father.

"I don't know. I just started to listen," he said, "with my heart."

LETTER TO THE EARTH

Dear Earth,

Give us the suffering we deserve. The pandemic you sent us is a beginning. Too often we have been saved by the benevolence of the universe. When salvation comes easily, we do not learn. We only learn through suffering. We have become too spoilt, too stupid, too self-regarding. We fancy ourselves as gods. But we are children of death and immortality. We are nothing but wonder woven into mortal flesh.

It is time for our flesh and our dreams to be tried. It is time for us to undergo the greatest initiation that we have undergone together as a species, an initiation of fire that brings us humility and illumination. We will not transform ourselves and be worthy of this fabled earth if we aren't raised up in some way. The only way is to temper us with fire and with iron.

I do not wish suffering on anyone. But the human race has failed in that solemn responsibility to fructify and enrich you, Earth, to add to your beauty, and evolve with you towards the fullest human possibilities.

We are not rising up to the greatness of the wonder woven in us.

We think we are only flesh and so our dreams are only of profit and dust. We think that there is no force anywhere capable of chastising us for our cruelties to you and to one another, our wars, our racism, our sexism, our injustices, our proliferation of poverty, our tormenting of the environment.

But there is a force which science does not understand. It is threaded into life itself, into the laws of physics and metaphysics. Some call it karma. I think of it as the natural tendency of the universe towards balance and harmony. This force is implicit in things. What we do will be done to us, the good and the bad.

We are receiving the fruits of the evils we have inflicted on you, Earth, and on one another. It all comes back to us. There is no need to have any emotion about this, for it happens as a condition of reality itself.

This baffles science. It confounds those who see only with the eyes.

But we are in an age of catastrophes. We initiated the catastrophes. We will receive what we deserve, receive it with lamentation and self-judgment.

Dear Earth, you inspire our dreams and our art. You feed our bodies and souls. You house our bones when we are gone. You are one of the terrestrial planets, made of the matter and magic of countless stars that have loaned you their magnificence that you may gift it to us.

Dear Earth, look kindly upon the folly that is the human race. Teach us with your silent wisdom how to live again, how to be simple again, and how to rise to the greatness and sense of universal justice that is our divine inheritance.

Yours lovingly,
Ben Okri

KERZE

It's out it's out
When it was lit
Light is out
Just freshly out
Out of time
Out of here
Gone up in smoke
Just gone out
Missed the moment
Missed the
When it's out it's out
When it's gone it's gone
Who can bring back
The missing light
Turn smoke back
Into fire
Turn back time
And the hour
Make it all light again
Kerze kerze kerze
Against the changing times.
First there was light
And it was good
In ritual or in the dark
Something to come home to
Something to see on a hill
In the night
When the sun is gone

And the moon's not out.
But now maybe the gods
Have done it
Or we are the gods
That did it to ourselves
Just did it within the motions
Of the clock
Where there are no shadows
Just the kerzesmoke
Where once there was flame
Or the absent flame
In the ghostly presence
Flame is concentrated
Smoke wavers and drifts
Sometimes the fire wavers
But throws its light
Into the far corners.
All the smoke can do is be
A ghost, a wisp, a regret,
Nostalgia, a wish undone,
Sometimes even an arch
Of floating spirits
Where the flames die together
In empty rooms.

Just thinking of those
Places
Where the shadows
Creep closer
And the darkness
Is given courage

And the spaces that
Had presences
Shrink and retreat
With the formless
Dark advancing
Not only in rooms
But in squares
In hearts
In dreams
In parks at noon
In parliaments
And the stock exchange
In schoolrooms
Where teachers are not free
In the bedrooms
Where the dark
Comes between
The warm bodies
Turning cold
In the streets
That used to lead
To the hill
But lead now
To the crossroads
Where lamps have gone
Out and the rats
Grow brave
In the undergrowth.

Can the smoke
Bring back the flame?

Does the flame survive
In the twisting form
Without a name?
Can that which is out
Be not out?
Can the dark
Extinguish itself
By itself?
Can the candle
Light itself?
Can the heart
Feel its own beat?
Can the feet
Smell the socks?
Are moths
Drawn to candlesmoke?
Can the light
Put out
Shine still
From that hill
Or among the flowers
On the windowsill?
Can we return
To the source?
Can the source return to us?
Can spilt sauce
Be unspilt?
Can spooled words
Be unspooled?
Can the candlesmoke
Illuminate

The cobwebs?
Can the darkness brighten
The walls
Where children
Read in silence
While the clock
Marks the time
In the dark?
Tick tock tick tock
It's out it's out
Keep your voice down
Don't shout
No one can hear you
When it's out
When the moon looms
And shadows
Advance across
The land
Tick tock tick tock
Listen to the clock
Ticking in the silent
Candle
On the mantelpiece
But look,
If you can see,
There's history
Expiring slowly
Slowly dancing
Writhing
Casting elegant
Shapes

In the fading
Dancing
Candlesmoke
But the end
Of things
Can be so beautiful
If anyone can see them

That sullen
Wisp
Of charm…

Keep it lit
While the song
Lasts…

Missed the moment
Missed the

AFTER THE END

1

It was a long night after the end. Many of us lived in the night and did not emerge. We knew nothing of what had happened except that one day everything went off. Everything shut down. The electricity was out and the internet no longer worked and none of the communication lines that ran the world existed anymore.

We learned to live in the dark, in houses under the ground, and in caves on the edges of the city. We had books and some of us read, for short periods of the day, with the light of improvised candles. No one went out into the air.

We were a community that lived now beneath the ground. We had forgotten what sunlight was. The air we breathed came through the tunnels in the earth, filtered by the earth itself. For many years we lived like this, pale and quiet, like human moles, unaware of what had been happening in the world above.

Over that time, beneath the ground, many of our families died. People can't endure being away from sunlight for long. Many perished of sun deprivation. Many simply wilted and surrendered themselves to the earth. Some of us tried to die but couldn't. I tried several times. I couldn't seem to find a way to die. After a while I came to accept the curse of life. Every day was an entombment. Every day the dream of light faded from our spirits. I would sleep at night but was unable to distinguish the night from the day. My dreams would be of nothing but sunlight. Sometimes I dreamt of fields of green. The green in my dreams was unnaturally alive. It made me weep to think of such a green. Sometimes I dreamt of rivers and streams, of running water. There was nothing as magical as the sun on my face in those dreams or the feeling of water splashed on my body.

It was down there that we began to reconstruct the world for ourselves. Having lost it, we tried to reconstruct it anew, from our nostalgia and our memories and our incomplete knowledge of the world. It was down there that I realized how little we knew of the world we had lived in before the night came down upon us. I regretted not having asked questions about the world, about how things worked, about the different peoples and their histories. We all realized down there that we had taken too much for granted about the world we had loved. Did we really love it, then, if we didn't know it? Can you love something you are quite ignorant about?

When we tried to recreate the world, we found that we could only recreate what we had known. We realized quickly that we were reconstructing our narrowness and our limitations. It was less than what we knew before. Therefore, we could not really begin again. And so we had to begin from nothing.

This was the hardest part. The more vocal among us wanted to rebuild what we had known. One said:

"The custom from my land is better. We once ruled the world. It stands to reason that our traditions must be the best."

"Your people ruled the world once? Well, my people ruled it last. We were more powerful than your people. It stands to reason that our ways are better than yours," said another.

Those of us who came from countries that hadn't ruled the world had the perfect answer for them.

"When you come to think about it," we said, "you people who ruled the world are in fact the ones who ruined it. Therefore, it stands to reason that your traditions and your ways are terrible models for the future. Your way led us here. Your way is not going to build a better future. It will just bring us back to this very same place, or worse."

"What could be worse than a living death?" said another, who came from people who had not ruled the world.

The women among us were not having any of it at all.

"None of you are in a position to speak. It was the masculine way that brought us to this darkness. The masculine way is not going to build any kind of future that we want."

As can be seen, we carried our past with us into the dark. At first, for a long time, that past held. People clung on to what they had been before as they would to a life raft. People talked about their homes and where they grew up with a nostalgia laced with tears. Those who had lost the most talked the most about what they had lost. Some of us didn't talk at all, but merely listened and watched.

In the beginning it did not seem as if being in the dark was going to be our fate. We thought we would be there for a short time and would eventually get a sign telling us that it was all clear in the world above and that we could return. But the sign never came. Some people, impatient to know what was going on in the world above, crept out through the tunnel into the light. Those who went to reconnoiter never came back. Not one of them. After the third party went and never returned, we began to fear that what was going on above was worse than we had imagined. No one went out there for a long time after that.

Up to that point everyone had treated their condition in the tunnel as provisional. They were sure that what had happened in the world would soon be over and that they could emerge and resume their old lives. Because of this thought, people held back and did not reveal much about themselves. But as soon as it became clear that they were stuck in the tunnel for the foreseeable future, people behaved differently and their will to dominate became apparent. Those who did not try to dominate at least tried to impose their ways on others. Groups formed and people clustered around those whose interests and backgrounds were similar to their own. What should have been a situation where everyone looked after each other soon became one in which groups looked after themselves. Then groups became antagonistic towards one another and before long were fighting over the little food that was available. The fights became vicious. It was not only the men who were fighting. The women too became wild and tough and sometimes were more frightening than the men.

It was because I found all this alarming, because I couldn't belong to any group – never having fitted in anywhere in my life – that I left the community and wandered deeper into the tunnel. Finding nothing there, I ventured out alone into what was left of the world.

As I was leaving, one of the women of the so-called alpha group saw me and gave a terrifying shriek. They were a group that had been the children of the heads of companies and high-powered organizations when the world was still functional. I was surprised that they got on with one another and that they didn't seek out weaker groups to dominate. But then perhaps they kept together because they were planning a kind of world domination for when the long night of terror was over. Anyway, the woman shrieked. Some men came after me, attempting to bring me back to the fold. But I ran with more urgency. I felt I would rather take my chances with a hostile world than with these intolerable egotists.

With these thoughts I ran beyond the walled territory that was the limit of the world of the tunnel. The men who had been sent to bring me back stopped there and watched me disappear. They didn't have the courage or the madness to transgress the line that marked the end of their territory. I had had enough. I would rather have died than stayed any longer with them. I ran into the old world that we all thought no longer existed.

I should have said that we had been living in the tunnels now for over seventy-five years. I was of the second generation. I had been raised on tales of how the world used to be, and how with greed and selfishness it was destroyed by some unspecified climate disaster, and was no longer fit for human habitation.

2

What I found outside the tunnels was a world renewed by our absence. I found a world that looked more like my parents' descriptions of a wild garden. There were patches of a curious white film over the earth. The trees grew in untamed profusion over the rough lands. Roads were no longer visible. Houses had been washed away. The landscape seemed to have been altered and rearranged in some extreme manner. I recognized nothing of the world I had been taught to know. There were birds in the air, but they bore no resemblance to any birds I had seen in books before. The woods rustled with strange small animals, but apart from that the world seemed uninhabited. I walked for a long time until I came to a place where tall structures could be seen in the distance. But when I got there, I saw that the structures were empty. They reached up to the sky, but they appeared to have no function. The doors that led into them were of steel and were bolted and rusted over, and this curious white film ran halfway up the structures.

Not far away were things that resembled houses. Some of the walls were still standing. In many of the houses, trees were growing, their branches sticking out of the side windows. I saw chimneys sprouting vines. What had once been gardens were now outposts of forests. The roads were broken up. Everything was derelict, but it seemed an inhuman dereliction. Ceiling after ceiling had collapsed. Chimneys were broken. A church was tilted sideways, as though beneath the earth its foundation had been rendered askew. Houses were sunk in wild tangles of vines and creepers.

I walked the roads and streets, and could see that somehow civilization had kept up its skeletal structures beneath the disorder wrought by time and the unknown devastation. Over most of this – the churches, the walls, the houses – was this white film.

I had been wandering round the city for most of the day when it occurred to me that the air was good. I forgot that I was breathing. I failed to notice that I had been in the world a whole day and that nothing had happened to me. That was when it occurred to me for the first time that life could begin anew.

My initial urge was to go back to the tunnel and tell those who were holed up there. Then I remembered all their attempts at bringing back an old domination, bringing back the old hierarchies, and I had my doubts. We don't need the way it *was* ruining how it could be, I thought. The old ways must die with the old world. To begin anew we must really begin anew. I decided to leave the others in the tunnel and never go back. It crossed my mind that this was perhaps why the others who had gone out before had not returned. But however far I traveled, I saw no evidence of any successful attempts to start life anew. I saw no signs of any previous survival. Still, I would keep alert.

I chose a house with a field next to it as the place to begin life anew. It was a sturdy house, completely empty, except for the furniture and some books and old sheaves of paper. It had a pantry devoid of food, a nice kitchen, a shed with all manner of tools, and bedrooms upstairs, some beds with ancient mattresses and some without. There was also a well-preserved library. The windows were shut, and most of the doors inside were open. I liked the house because from its first-floor windows you could see all around. It was built on a slight rise. From the south-facing windows you could see the field running all the way to the copse and beyond it to the woods. Something about the landscape made me feel there was a stream in those woods.

The mood in the house was old and moldy and subdued. The doors were all still working, but there was mold in the downstairs rooms, and the basement door was jammed. There was no electricity. There was no water. There were taps, but I didn't know how to work them. The garden had become a lush little patch of wildness at the back of the house. The smell of mice was everywhere.

3

When I left the world of the tunnel, I brought nothing with me. What could I have brought? How do you prepare for a world which you don't even know is there? The house seemed to have everything I would need, but I simply didn't know how most things worked. The world outside the tunnel had been nothing but a rumor to me all my life. I had read books and listened to the older ones, who had listened to their parents, who remembered something of what it was like. I had learned one thing from them: never to follow the route they had taken. They talked with affection about gardening, about travel, about large parties, about schools, universities, careers, adventures, money, success, music festivals, falling in love. I asked one of the oldest ones what she missed most about the world outside the tunnel, and she said:

"Being young in the spring."

I had no idea what she meant, and she didn't elaborate. But she went on to say something else:

"Our biggest mistake," she said, "is that we were in too much of a hurry. We evolved more in a hundred years than we had in the one hundred thousand years before that. We ate up everything so fast we even started devouring our own entrails. If we ever have the chance to do it over again, we should slow down. We should learn to enjoy one thing for a long time. But first we should get rid of the spirit of competition."

"Why would you do that? I thought people said it was what made us so great?"

"But then it fed into our greed, and our greed finally devoured the planet."

"But what would you put in its place?"

"Collaboration. It comes from laboring together."

"But can we really do that? Are we not programmed to compete, to be greedy, to want to win?"

"We did that programming to ourselves and then made it essential to our culture. But we can be many things, not just one. When we build together, it is better than when we build alone."

Those conversations, those fears, were the things I brought with me to the world beyond the tunnel.

The first day in the house, I could not sleep. The night was full of voices. They were the voices of the wild. Everywhere in the city nature had returned and reclaimed its fertile terrain. At night the rewilded world spoke and sang and called and whistled. The wind blew among the trees that had grown everywhere, grown in the middle of cathedrals and churches, sprouted on the roofs of houses, their roots stretching down from the ceiling to touch the earth. Deer and hares and wild boars that were thought to have long vanished from the land roamed free in the cities, which were now their terrain. At night I heard lions coughing far away, and sometimes the chattering of apes reminded me of the ceaseless arguments that got out of hand in the world of the tunnel, after which one of those involved would retreat and not be seen for weeks.

I had never known what it was like to sleep away from people, in a world wild and unknown. I had chosen a room upstairs to sleep in because there was something resembling a bed there. I slept on wooden boards, and had nothing to cover me except the clothes I had brought. It was cold at night, and I shivered long into my dreams. In the depth of the night, I heard rustlings downstairs, but I did not get up to investigate. Those rooms were now the terrain of whatever had made this their home in the place of humans. I had no intention of usurping their world.

In the morning I found animal droppings in the living room, but no animals were around. After looking everywhere to make sure I was safe, I set about making the house habitable. Windows that were broken, I boarded up. I cut a path to the stream. I weeded the garden. I lived off simple foods, off vegetables in the garden and all around the houses. I cleared up the road. Sometimes while I worked, I had the distinct sense that I was being watched. But it wasn't by human beings. I knew the weight and the heat of human eyes that watch you. Deer had left tracks everywhere, and I was tempted to hunt them for meat. But I refrained. I reasoned that they had reclaimed the city for themselves and were now living in mysterious balance with nature, and it wasn't for me to come and ruin it. In the kitchen I found an instrument that gave off sparks and with it I made a fire. I found chickens running free and lived off their eggs, which I took judiciously. At night I lit a lamp and bolted all the doors. Upstairs in my room I would read in the absolute solitude of night.

There were moments when I felt I was in a dream. Then I would wake and find myself in what I thought was a nightmare. But it wasn't so bad after all. I didn't much miss other people. Maybe it was because their spirit, the society they had made, the end of time they had created, was all around me in the silence of a world without man or woman or child. The wonder is that not everything was erased. We thought that it had all been wiped clean off the face of the earth, and that the earth would get a chance to begin anew, as after a great and final apocalypse, or a universal fire burning away every last trace of humanity. That's what the tunnels were for: so we would survive the destruction of everything. But then we brought our toxic past with us. I just had to get away from the destructive logic of humans. I didn't miss other people. Their history, in ruins, was all around me.

And so I began again on my own, surrounded by wolves and wild beasts and large rodents and horses wandering the cities looking for food. I stayed in the house, and after many weeks I brought some order to it and made the garden nice and built a fence to keep out the wolves. Every night I lit a fire and roasted a chicken or a rabbit. Often I stared into the fire and mused about an alternative history of the human race – if we are ever given the chance of a new Eden.

4

I lived like this for weeks and months, and I think I was happy. I had no time to wonder about it. I worked hard all day and fell into sleep as you might dive into a warm sea in the height of summer. I slept better in that momentous solitude than I ever had. And then one day, after I had gone for a walk down the road to see what new vegetables I could bring back to my garden, I heard someone or something crying. I thought I had imagined it and stopped walking to listen. The sound continued, and it took a while to trace it. Then I saw its source, on the steps of a house that had crumbled to dust. Metal rods were sticking out of the foundation, but the steps were still there, keeping their structure.

And there she was, like a figure I had seen in a long-ago magazine. She wore blue trousers, a yellow shirt, and had a cloth wound round her head. She was like a mirage or a hallucination, a dream sent by some deity to tempt me out of the oceanic solitude in which I had been luxuriating. I stared at her awhile, unable to move or think. I didn't want to frighten her, so I kept still. Then suddenly she stood up.

"Who is there?" she asked. "I can feel human eyes on me. Who is it? Show yourself!"

Then I stepped out into what was left of the square. Now it was her turn to stare at me, her mouth half open.

"Who are you?" she asked. "And how do you come to be here? Are you a ghost, a devil, a dream? Are you real? You can't be real, you're not speaking. I'm imagining you, aren't I? I've gone crazy, haven't I?"

She began weeping again.

"You haven't gone crazy," I said gently. "And I am real. Question is, are you real?"

She didn't say anything for a moment. Then, giving a sudden cry, she got up and ran out of the square faster than I imagined possible. A moment later there was absolutely no sign that she had been there, that she was real and not just a figment of my tremendous solitude. I went in the direction she had gone and saw no one. I spent the rest of the day wandering around, trying to find her, but she was nowhere to be found and left no sign of her existence whatsoever. At last I went back to the house, but there was now a new uneasiness in my spirit.

I couldn't stop thinking about her. She had appeared there out of the altered air, like a genie, or a vision. If she was real, this made it harder to fathom. Was she in this world by herself? Had she been by herself all along? Why did she run from me? Is she with others? Can there be more people out there? Why hadn't I seen them? I had been everywhere in the empty city and seen no sign of new life at all, no sign of the unmistakable presence of humans.

All night I tossed and turned, unable to get the apparition out of my mind. I came to the conclusion that what I had seen was the image my mind wanted me to see, a compensation for the solitude in which I dwelt. I had read how Antarctic explorers in past centuries had seen among their number someone who wasn't there. I had heard of women having fugitive visions of vanished peoples. It was said that certain places often conjured up the ghosts of those who had lived there long before. Maybe landscapes yield trace memories of people. Maybe squares dream of those who have played and laughed there. Maybe fountains relive the laughter of children who have jumped around in them. But then maybe I had gone so long now without seeing anyone that, for my sanity's sake, my mind was inventing a girl for me. As I lay in bed, I could see her. I was talking to her when darkness invaded me, and before I knew it dawn was at the window, looking in.

5

I did not see her the next time I went to the square. I wasn't expecting to see her. But I kept my senses open. It was a lovely day in spring. The utter dereliction of the city, the fallen masonry, the broken columns, the crumbling steps of public buildings, the strange white substance that had discolored everything, the flowers and plants that grew all along the pavements and on the roads, the trees that had grown through the concrete of houses and squares, the cracked tiles of diplomatic quarters, the empty palaces where royalty had once commanded the adoration of the multitudes, the school buildings taken over by masses of birds, the police stations overrun by wild boars and growling mastiffs, the tall telecommunications tower that was now nothing but a symbol of the failed age of digital hopes – all were now refreshed by the emergence of spring.

The fine light of the sun made the ruination of the city strangely forlorn and charming. No one had ever seen it like this before. No one could have imagined that this would be its fate. There were no human voices in the squares, now teeming with weeds and bright, flaming flowers. Mushrooms of a particularly deadly-looking hue mounted the walls of Parliament. And the House of Lords was buried, like a dark enchantment, beneath a forest of ivy so thick that it seemed almost impenetrable.

I wandered through the lonely city and did not see a soul. I heard no strange sounds, except the sounds of birds and animals wandering freely on the bridge. All the buildings, the roads and pavements, the rooftops and chimneys, and even the spires and the tall towers were covered with this white film. When I scraped it, the film would not come off. I sometimes had to chip at it. I could make no sense of the taste. It tasted like nothing I ever knew.

I walked far into the city with the hope of stumbling upon the girl again. Birds had taken up residence in several houses. Monkeys from the zoo chattered in the upper balcony of a church. Every now and again a horse would bolt through the streets, startling me. Nowhere did I see any sign of a living human being. Disappointed, I went back home. I kept up this search for another week, with the same results. By the end of the week, I became uncertain of what the girl looked like. Two weeks later I could not really be sure if I had seen her at all. By the end of a month, I gave up altogether.

But it made me think about what I would do if I did meet another human soul in this wilderness of a world.

6

In the meantime, I continued working on my garden. I borrowed plants from the whole city. Flowers grew everywhere, indiscriminately. Marigolds grew beside giant rhubarb, poinsettias next to nettles, wild roses beside geraniums. I saw flowers I had never heard of before. I brought the ones I liked back with me. I made a garden out of nothing. It was how I made the time useful. In the evenings, after cooking food for myself, I would read. The city was one vast sprawling library, and I brought back books from my expeditions. I found books in empty houses, in broken libraries, in royal collections. In many places books were moldering, their paper turning to mush. In one house the books had sprouted red-and-cardamom-colored mushrooms. One book I opened dissolved upon contact with the atmosphere. It was the strangest thing. It was entirely intact till I opened it, and then its words became dust and air. It made quite a troubling impression on me as I walked back to the house over the bridge and along the roads where houses had dissolved to piles of dust and rubble.

As I neared my house, I had an uncanny sense of

something not quite right. It nagged away at me. There was a field near the house with lime and ash trees. They were huge, their branches solid, their leaves lush for that time of year. I always stopped to look at them when I went past. But that day there was something unusual about them, something that bothered me about them that I could not identify. I looked at the trees, at the branches, and saw some wrens' nests. I had just turned my head away and was about to go through the fence gate when I realized what was different. I looked again, and there she was, sitting with her back against the ash tree, asleep. She must have silently tracked me down.

I stared at her in wonder for a full three minutes until I saw that she was now awake. She looked as though she had been awake all along. She didn't move when she saw me. She just stared. I didn't know what to do, so I stayed where I was, with the pile of books under my arms.

"So, you found me," I said at last.

"I wasn't looking," she said.

"Then why are you here?"

"To lay down ground rules."

"What for?"

"Us."

"Why?"

"I know you've been trying to find me."

"How many of you are there?"

"None of your business." She paused, then said, "Only me."

"If it's just us, don't you think we should work together?"

"We have to find a new way to do this or it's not going to work. I will disappear and you will never see me again."

137

"Okay. I don't want that."

"Good."

"Do you want to come in?"

"That's how it begins. So, no. Let's talk here on neutral territory."

I began to walk towards her.

"Stop. Not another step or you'll never see me again."

I stopped. She hadn't really looked at me all this time. Her back was still calmly against the tree. There was something unsettling about her presence there. It was as if she were a nature spirit made visible, some kind of ghostly form that had emerged from the tree itself. Her colors were green and brown and her mood serene, almost indifferent. Her self-possession was uncanny.

"We are not going to do it the way it was done before."

"Do what?"

"All of it. I've been reading about all of it. That was the only way to make sense of how all this came to be, this ruination of a world. We are not doing what was done before."

"Then what are we doing?"

"I don't know. But as far as I can see, this is a new beginning. Or an end. Maybe it's too late to begin. But we can't give up and do nothing. So we must find a way to begin even if it's too late to begin. Because history is over. And we are the fag end of it."

"I like that you say 'we.'"

"I'm not including you in this 'we.'"

"Oh."

"That's what I came to tell you. Keep to your space. Don't encroach on mine. I don't want any romance or any kind of union that becomes a form of power relations. I don't want to be your wife or anything like that. You manage your world as you see fit, and I will manage mine as I see fit. And don't fall in love with me. Love in the end did nothing for the human race. They loved and still they brought the whole thing crashing down. They actually managed to bring about the end of everything just by the way they lived and loved. If we are to survive, we have to find something else."

"What?"

"I don't know. But while I'm trying to figure it out, I don't want anything to complicate it. I want the complete freedom to think. I don't want my time to be affected by you in any way."

"My time is already affected by you, whether I see you or not. You are now a part of my breathing and my dreams."

"Don't do that."

"What?"

"Imprison me with love. Your idea of love."

"What have you got against love?"

"It begins as love and ends as power."

"Why? It doesn't have to. Not if it's real love."

"I haven't come to debate such antiquated notions with you."

"What have you come for then?"

"To tell you to leave me alone."

"But we are the only two people left. We may as well work together in some way. We won't survive if we don't work together."

"What makes you think I want to survive?"

"You're still here, aren't you?"

"Still here. But not for want of trying."

She stood up in a single fluid motion. I was not sure how she did it.

"Keep to your domain and I'll keep to mine. Run your world the way you want, and I'll run mine the way I want. Do you get it?"

"Yes," I said.

Then she was gone. I didn't see how she went. She seemed to dissolve into the trees, like mist. I stood there a long time, looking at the spot where I had last seen her. Perhaps I was hoping that she would return, or that she had never left. But she was gone, and I knew I would not see her for a long time.

7

My loneliness was worse afterwards. For days I kept listening for her. I would look at the foot of the tree and imagine that she was there. But it was only a trick of the shadow or the force of my longing creating an image of her out of the movement of light on the leaves. I avoided the parts of town where I suspected she might be. My garden grew luxuriant. Soon I had gathered most of the flowers that could be found in the city. Foxes were everywhere, but they didn't bother me. Wolves had drifted in from the countryside, and sometimes I heard animals fighting for their territories. I heard the snapping of jaws at night, and the howling and the snarling of beasts defending their broods.

After a lot of time passed and I didn't see her again, I wondered if she was still alive. It was in those times that I felt the arrangement she insisted on was not practical. Whether she was alive or not mattered to me. To be alone again after having discovered that she was in the world seemed unbearable. So one morning I sought her out, if only to know whether she was dead or not.

It took me most of the day, but I came to a street that looked different from all the others. Flowers lined the edges of the pavement. I followed the flowers till I came to the house. It was a modest Regency-style house, but there were wooden sculptures everywhere. There was a beautiful garden of the happiest-looking flowers. I went up to the door and knocked. I didn't hear anything. Then I went in. The door, surprisingly, was open. I found her on the sofa, lying down, with a dull look in her eyes.

"I was hoping you would have the good sense to ignore what I said and come and find me. I am glad you came."

"What's wrong?"

"I have a nasty cold."

"You need someone to look after you."

"And will you do that?"

"Yes, with pleasure."

"Why?"

Knowing how touchy she was about love, I did not know what to say. She was watching me closely.

"See, you have no reason. You're just…"

"Lonely?"

"Yes, that's it."

"I'm not lonely. I've got the birds and the trees."

"What is it then?"

"Why are you hostile towards having anything to do with me?"

"I'm not. It's just that I don't want history to repeat itself."

"What history?"

"All of it." She paused. "We have to make a new history, or we'll just start the same cycle of creation and destruction that brought us to this point."

For the first time I heard what she was saying. She was right. It is as if the logic of being human is tilted in a certain direction, as if we can't escape what we are. We are doomed to compete, to exploit, to conquer, to control, to make hierarchies, to make power structures out of differences, to make power structures out of everything.

"But how are we going to be different from what we've been in the past," I asked, "when human nature seems so flawed?"

"We have to have agreements. We have to reshape human nature," she said.

"Can it be done?"

"We weren't always what we became. That happened over time."

"What's the first thing you would propose?"

"Equality," she said.

"But how can you propose equality without the power to enforce it?"

"Do I need power to enforce it?"

"Not with me, but with others."

"Once power enters the picture, then we are lost," she said.

"But power is always there."

"That's why I want my domain and you can have yours."

"But you are sick now and need someone. Another time it could be me. We need one another. Do you want to be absolutely on your own?"

"Might not be so bad." She paused. "No. I wouldn't."

"What about if we banish power?" I said, suddenly inspired.

"How do we do that? The first oafish person from the tunnels to see the world all empty and fresh again will want to take it over and rule. Then we are going to need power to deal with him or her. So we will always need power to deal with the impulse of power when it arises."

"So what are we to do then?"

"We will make new laws. The first new laws of the race to come after us."

"What will your first law be?"

"Every person is an inviolate and unique being. No one's humanity is to be diminished in any way."

"Is that a law or a saying?"

"It's the best I can do with this nasty cold I've got. Look, thank you for coming round. But can we do this another day?"

I had offered to look after her, but now I could tell she wanted me gone. Perhaps the fact that I had found her was enough for the moment. I left straightaway, and she did not look up as I was leaving.

8

I stayed away for a week, then I brought flowers, hoping that she was better. She didn't answer the door. As I was leaving, I heard her call me from an upper room.

"You didn't have to kill a couple of flowers for me."

"I didn't kill them," I said defensively. "I just cut them."

She came down and sat on a sofa. She was looking better, with a bright scarf round her neck.

"Imagine someone cutting your flower to give away as a gift."

"Their flowers will grow back; mine won't. That's the difference."

"That's going to be one of my laws."

"What?"

"There must be respect for all life."

"Can we respect plants and animals and eat them?" I asked.

"If you respect them, why eat them?"

"Fair question, but plants have no emotions. They don't feel pain."

"How do you know?"

"They would cry out if they did."

"So crying is the only way of knowing whether a being feels pain? That is so human-centric. What if they felt and expressed pain another way? What if an alien species who expresses pain by turning green subjected us to various torments and we didn't turn green? They would be justified in concluding that we felt no pain and forever afterwards could subject us to unmentionable tortures."

"What are you saying?"

"We have to respect the rights of forests and trees and plants and flowers."

"Won't nature be wild then, and unmanageable?"

"As opposed to exploited and dead?"

"Your world is becoming impossible," I said.

"And the world as you see it is already extinct. Don't you get it, those of us who have survived must take the human race in a new direction or we will make the same mistakes again."

"But can the human race be taken in a new direction?"

"Right now, *we* are the human race. Can we go in a new direction?"

I stood thinking about it for a long time.

"Will you have children?"

"I don't want to."

"Why not?"

"For all the reasons I've been giving. If we can't take ourselves in a new direction, then there's no point in having kids."

"But we have to have kids or there will be nothing."

"Is that such a bad thing?"

"What? I can't believe you are saying that. Of course it's a bad thing."

"Why?"

"This is our planet. Humans should be here. It's ours too."

"Is it? Is it really yours? How is it yours? All the other species were here long before you arrived on the scene. We are just latecomers who took over the party. We overextended our reach and made ourselves extinct. Here we are, living in the aftermath of humanity, and we're still hankering for the things that brought about our demise. Are we not mad? This book I was reading made me think. Is humanity a preparatory species, doomed by its inherent limitations to be a forerunner to a wiser species that will transcend our fatal errors and make this earth the paradise it was always meant to be?"

"You think we are just a bridge to something else, something higher?"

"Yes. The more I think of our history, the more I conclude that we are just a rehearsal for the real act that will come after us. We were a warm-up show. We are flawed forerunners. Like the Atlanteans were before we came along."

"And where will they come from, the real act to which we are forerunners?"

"I don't know. They will come from elsewhere. Like us, they will have lost their planet, having taken all their blessings for granted. They will have been searching the galaxies for millennia, looking for a place of beauty that can sustain their life forms. Maybe it is they to whom the paradise of the earth is promised, because we have been disastrous caretakers of the miracle. I don't know. It's just a conjecture. Maybe even a fantasy."

"But what about us?"

"Us?"

"You and I?"

"We can't start a new earth."

"Why not?"

"Because I don't want to. I don't think we deserve a

second chance. I don't trust the impulse of human history that is in me."

"But we're different. If we work together, we can start an entirely new history."

"I don't want to think about it. I want to sleep now."

She shut her eyes. I left. A week later she came to see me. She found me in the garden. She had been watching me for a while before I noticed her. I had felt the critical weight of her eyes, but could not place it.

"I've been watching you," she said. "You work as if you are expecting a mate."

"What do you mean?"

"Why are you taking such trouble with your garden? You wouldn't take such trouble if you were all alone in the world. There would be no point."

I was silent. I realized that nothing I said would ever persuade her. I had come to accept that she wanted nothing to do with me. I represented for her everything that had gone before. She represented for me all that was to come. I kept silent and brought her drinks and avoided looking into her face.

"I had a dream last night that you died and that I was all alone here," she said. "All the plants and trees and birds and sky started talking to me, and their speech was so big and strange that it frightened me, and I woke up with a jump. A world without you is worse than I imagined."

I said nothing. I went back to work. I was clearing the leaves, smoothing the hedges, and generally keeping the garden clean and fine-looking. Why was I doing it? No one was going to see it. Least of all her. I had given up on her.

"I think you're right. We have to do something or one day one of us will be horribly alone in an empty world. Just makes me tremble to think of it."

I began to water the lilies and begonias.

"Are you giving me the silent treatment?"

"You criticize the human past, and yet you behave selfishly and irrationally yourself," I said. "You want to do what suits you. Then you want to change your mind when it suits you too. It seems to me that we are ill-matched; I accept that we are doomed, and that's fine with me. I'd rather live in peace and be lonely than be subjected to your endless games. If we are wiped out, then so be it. At least let me have some peace."

She stared at me a long time. Then she vanished into the bushes and was gone. I could hear her footsteps far away. Two weeks passed and I didn't see her. I thought it best to forget her. I worked my garden. Then I wrecked it. Then I started again. I had fits of weeping that lasted two days. I screamed into the trunk of lime trees. I found a gun in the house, along with bullets, and wanted to kill the wolves that marauded the woods near me. I starved myself for three days and was quite willing to let the world die with me. On the fourth day, as I lay on the kitchen floor, with everything becoming more blurred around me, I saw this angelic form hovering over me, and I passed out in its light. Then it was darkness.

And then my head ached. A harsh sunlight shone into the house, and it seemed as if I had missed a whole season. When I tried to move, I couldn't. I could barely keep my eyes open. I became aware that someone had been feeding me. After what seemed like two days, I heard the song of the lark above the far roof. I heard something cracking in the earth. I found these ominous sounds oddly restful. A day later, emaciated, I sat up and looked around.

She was sitting across from me, watching me with intense eyes. When I moved, I could feel her move too, but subtly. I settled my eyes on her a long time and did not speak. I did not know what to say. She smiled.

"Is there any way we can start again?" she said.

"From what?"

"From where we went wrong. I went wrong. I was being an individualist. I was putting my concerns about power above everything else. Then I saw that if I am here in this world on my own, it becomes meaningless whether I have my own power or not. I don't want to be queen of the world if it means being on my own in the world."

"Is that what you really want? To be queen of the world?"

"Perhaps! Maybe underneath all my posturing that's what I really want! Quite shocking, isn't it?" she said, pretending to look shocked.

"Quite," I said, wearily. "But you are queen of the world."

"Because I am the only woman! Not very hard, is it?" she laughed. "How are you feeling?"

"Surprised that I am still here."

"Please be here. It is truly frightening being here on my own. Last night a pack of wolves howled outside my window. I had the weird impression that they were camped there, waiting for me. I couldn't sleep a wink. I heard sounds all over the house, and I was convinced they had got in and were coming to eat me alive. Do you think love originated in the primal loneliness of our ancestors?"

I grunted. Twice. She got the joke, and smiled.

"It's a long way from that loneliness to the wars and terminal egotism of our last civilization. It seems our people lost their way a very, very long time ago."

I said nothing. I was happy to hear her voice and her thoughts.

"I never told you how I got here," she said. "And I will never tell anyone else. Our people lived in the far north of the tunnels. Been living there now for over half a century. I think at some point we began to go mad. There's no other way to describe what happened. Every now and again someone would try to take over the group. There was nothing to take over, we were living in holes; yet someone would try and take over, and give orders, and take the women for themselves, and the rest of us would have to fight them. People got killed. It is as if people, in the extreme isolation in which we were living, suddenly became power crazy. It was as if power was the only thing that could console them after the destruction of the world, as if the misery of our lives could only be compensated for by power over others.

"I swore then, when I was a child, that I would always be free, even if it killed me. It nearly killed me being unfree. One uncle seized the women and wanted them as his concubines. He claimed to be the strongest. Fights broke out and relations were killed by relations. People had power fights over everything: over the women, the food, prime sections of the tunnel, and, above all, the light.

"We only had two hours of sunlight a day in the tunnels where we lived, and power determined who got to be in that sunlight. It poured in from a crack no larger than an egg, but that light became what most of us lived for. The most powerful had the first light. They stood under it and basked in it and washed their faces in the beam. Then it was their wives and children. And after them the next most powerful ones took in the light. Often, fatal combats broke out about who should stand in the light. Many of us went for months, even years, without ever standing in the light. All we could do was watch the beam from afar, watch it on the heads of those who were powerful enough to deprive us of it.

"A time came when my father was unable to take it anymore. He could no longer bear living in the darkness of the tunnel, able to see the beam of light but never to taste it or feel it on his face. One morning he dared to go to the crack in the tunnel before anyone else and lift his face up to the first rays of light. The joy this gave him was extraordinary to behold. But his act so angered the powerful ones among us that they struck my father on the head with a jagged stone, and I saw the crown of blood on his head, which the beam of light illuminated. The blood ran down his face and collected in his eyes. The look on his face suggested that his martyrdom was worth feeling, after all those years in the dark, that heavenly light on his face. Even if it was just once. He died that night. Two days later, in a way that had become almost normal in the tunnels, my mother willed her own death.

"After we buried her, many things happened too terrible to tell which woke in me the resolve to escape and face the certain death of the outside world rather than live another day an eternal prisoner of mindless power. It wasn't a desire for light or for life that drove me out. It was the desire to be free, to never again be tyrannized, to never let anyone condemn me to darkness while they keep all the light.

"As you can see, my history has not predisposed me to accommodate others. But I see now that drawing extreme conclusions from my experiences, no matter how bitter and terrible, is not much better than depriving others of light. We can learn the wrong lessons from what happened to us. I did, and I'm sorry. You are not a tunnel tyrant. At least I hope not. Please let's start again."

"How?"

"Tell me how you came to be here."

I told her the little I could in the manner that my poor strength allowed, in a low voice, with no inflection. She listened to me with vacant eyes, more silent than she had ever been.

"So the people from your tunnel are still there?"

"I don't know."

"Are you tempted to go and tell them that there is still a world out here?"

"No."

"Why not?"

"Same reason as you. They will revert back to what they were before. Within fifty years they will replicate the same conditions that brought us here. I fear them more than the bubonic plague I read about. Leave them in their ignorance."

"That's what I think. I also think that we must look after one another. After all, we are all we've got."

"Is that a new principle of yours?"

"I have many new principles."

9

When I got better and could walk and take in the sun, I found that I did not recognize her anymore. She seemed an entirely different person. She was always smiling. She no longer spent all her time in her house. She seemed not so keen to be alone anymore.

Together we rebuilt my garden, which had become a little ruined while I was ill. Foxes and other wild creatures had torn their way through it. There was something odd about the way the garden was shredded. We started having big fires in the nights to keep wild animals away. We found wood everywhere. The houses, though crumbling, had stores of all manner of things that had survived whatever had befallen the world while we were in the tunnels. We found supplies of candles. We found an old electric generator. It took us a week to drag it back to the house, and a month to get it to work. We found guns and bullets. In a run-down museum we found a cannon and an old machine gun. We found cellars full of wine from many centuries ago. Some of the bottles of wine had preserved so wonderfully that when we uncorked them, their fragrance filled the living room and their fruity taste, redolent of long tranquil summers, lingered on the palate and in the mind for days. Some bottles held only ancient wine-dust.

The cellars of the city yielded tools, boots, a fruit-pressing machine, computers, cords, weighing machines, records, clothes, parts of cars – in short, all the equipment that was used to sustain a household. Every day we brought back something new.

We shared everything equally. We agreed that we must not allow one to have more than the other. We agreed that we were mutually dependent. It was in the interest of the one that the other was healthy and alive. Labor too must be shared. No one was allowed to sit down while the other worked. No one was a servant. No one's status was higher than the other's. The land was held in common. Love was voluntary. No one was obliged to love back. Day after day we added to these principles, which the extreme gravity of our situation compelled us to discover. Everyone deserves respect. Everyone has the right to be heard, even if they have nothing to say. Everyone has to make their contribution to the running of things. We agreed quite quickly that money would not be a part of the world we were making from scratch.

"But how do we measure value then?" I asked.

"We measure value by how things enrich our lives," she said with that clarity of hers which was at once considered and light.

She took to writing the principles down on a board.

"But what if we don't know how to measure the value of something? We might think something valueless, when its value is in its absence."

"Example?"

That was her way. Whenever I said anything that was abstract, she asked for an example, to concretize my thinking.

"Peace," I said.

"That's because you think peace is passive. But I think peace is dynamic."

"Really? You're bringing a special meaning to the word."

"I think peace is the result of active qualities like forethought, hard work, vigilance. Peace is not for me the absence of discord, but the fruit of cultivation."

"What about beauty? What does beauty actually do?"

"Beauty is not passive. Beauty inspires. It makes us think. It gives us ideals. It makes us want to be better, in some way."

"Strange you should say that. Beauty makes me surrender. It brings me to the edge of the impossible. It often fills me with despair."

"What are you talking about?"

"I'm not sure."

Then she gave me an untranslatable look and stomped off out of the house and was gone for a day or so. When she was gone like that, I would just sit in the garden or in the room and stare out of the window, my mind vacant, the huge emptiness of the city crowding down on me. In times like that a crack from the abyss would enter my mind. I would become aware of the whole world and its vacancy, and a terror would come over me that would paralyze me for days. And it was only the sound of wolves outside – jostling in the streets below, or warring with the other beasts that now prowled the countryside and the towns – that roused me from my existential torpor.

On one such day, as I waited for something to wake me up from the funk in which I was wallowing, I heard the sound of weeping coming from the trees over on the south side of the house. I sought out the place and found no one. But the weeping sound continued. Then I concluded that perhaps it was a fugitive feature of the place. I think I was right in this because a day later the sound of weeping came from somewhere else; and it went on moving each day, till one day it was far across the city, and then it moved on, out into the world.

10

She returned one afternoon looking very thin. It was as if the emptiness of the world were erasing her. She told me she had seen a green cloud drifting towards us. I was going to ask her about it when she said, as if she'd been brooding on it a long time in solitude:

"In the new world we are making, everyone ought to have the same quality of education."

"What about those who don't want to be educated?"

"We have to change what education means. It shouldn't be something you are compelled to do, like going to school every day. It should be conveyed as a tool for life. That's what it should be."

"Tools for living?"

"Yes. A book I read in the tunnels said that in the past most people were not educated at all. Many were educated to fail. Only a few were educated to succeed. That's all wrong. Everyone should be educated to live. Education ought to be a basic human right, like eating, or sleeping."

"And you want everyone to have the same standard of education?"

"Yes. Everyone should know how to start a fire, build a house, survive on an island, craft a boat, give birth, sew up a wound, read directions by the stars... In short, everyone ought to be a mini-civilization. So that when the world perishes, and one person is left—"

"In our case, two."

"Then they should, together, be able to start civilization all over again, but better."

I was puzzled about why she was talking like this. She had a strange new passion in her spirit. Her eyes were ablaze when she spoke.

"We should teach children to read the world, to know about animals and plants and trees, to know what is poisonous, and how to neutralize poisons. We should teach them how to know people, to read their characters. They should read nature. Sooner or later they will create science again, but it should be an enlightened science: not one that wants to shut down and abolish the mysteries, but one that wants to reveal them, and thus amplify them; not a science that is an enemy to the spirit of human beings, but an ally; not one that is afraid of not having the answers, but one that relishes the questions and the unknown."

"I would like a science that explores the mystery of what we are," I said. "Did you know that once, for a brief period, science actually proved the reality of telepathy? But other scientists were apparently so threatened by this unknown thing that they ridiculed the findings. I was surprised to hear that science was every bit as close-minded as the church.

"The church took three hundred and fifty years to acknowledge that Galileo was right. But science never allowed itself to acknowledge that telepathy might be right, and that things have an aura, that thoughts travel through space, that objects hold memories. Science has its own flat-earth adherents when it comes to the mysteries."

I had been talking for a while when I realized that she was silent. I looked at her. There was a puzzled expression on her face. I felt that I was boring her, or that I was wearying her, so I got up and left the room. I went out to the garden and sat in a chair and watched the green cloud drifting ever closer.

After a moment she came out to the garden and sat next to me. She sat really close. Her proximity terrified me. Her intelligence was like a consuming fire. She was staring straight ahead, but something about her was burning me. I got up and walked away from her towards the laurel bush. She gave me a look that was like a flash of anger. I looked away from her, up to the sky, at the green cloud approaching. It hovered over about a quarter of the faraway sky. I was staring at it when I heard her coming towards me. I wanted to run. Her energy was overwhelming, even from yards away. There was a fence nearby, and I began, irrationally, to climb it. I got over, stumbled through the ragged rose bushes, and made it to the wildly overgrown street beyond. The mood she was in seemed like a madness. I don't know why it frightened me so suddenly. I'd felt the same sort of fear in the emptiness of the city, with no human life around, just the insurgent trees splitting the squares and the climbing vines suffocating the buildings and obscuring the churches till nothing could be seen but this century-old takeover of the city, its palaces and government offices, its fountains and cinemas. That's the terror I felt near her.

I walked along for a while and made my way back through the tangle of bushes that was the street. I found her sitting where I had last seen her, with a dreamy expression in her eye.

"Why are you afraid of me?" she asked.

I looked at her. Did she really mean that question?

"You have a sharp intelligence," I said. "But it's like an old chainsaw – you don't know what you cut, or what you decapitate."

"Am I that bad?"

"Not bad at all. It's just that your equipment is more powerful than your consciousness."

She looked crestfallen.

"Nobody wants me," she said.

"Nobody wants to be lectured at all the time," I said, and felt ashamed of it.

"I promise I won't lecture you again," she said.

I went over to her, not wanting to seem intimidated. Her eyes widened as I approached. Then she caught my arm and, with a lazy swaying gesture, said:

"You're strong. When did you become so strong?"

"Am I strong? I'm not so sure. Sometimes I—"

"I always admired your strength."

"Really?" I found myself backing away. There was something panther-like about her swinging, swaying mood. Was she toying with me?

"How you can be here by yourself, alone in all the world. That's strength."

"Or disgust with the others."

"A sense of disgust is strength too."

I looked into her eyes. For a moment I could not see the person I had seen before. A new person stood before me, but I could not trust my eyes.

"Let's start everything again. Let's begin again at the beginning. I was a little mad before, but I'm better now. It's like something has swept the sickness out of my head. I feel new. I am ready for a new—"

She lowered her head. Then she began, silently, to weep. I felt heartless and miserable watching her. My fear of her moods stopped me going towards her for a moment. Then I realized that nothing in the world was ever going to happen again if I didn't get past my fear, my doubt, or the love that I had buried deep in my pride, buried and smothered. Nothing was ever going to happen again. The flowers wouldn't be the same, and the green cloud would conquer the sky, and the tunnels would find a way to open up right in the midst of our immemorial solitude. All of the past, with its tragic arc, would live again if I did not find a way to cross the abyss that shone between us. She stopped weeping, stood up, and began walking away from the garden. She paused at the tall roses, red and fleshy and bright in the afternoon sun. She began moving again, past the roses, and I said:

"Wait!"

She turned eyes of pure clarity towards me and held me with a question. The look in her eyes restored me to a self I had never known, gave me to my new self. I was changing as I walked towards her, all my uncertainty gone, and I understood now the meaning of that green cloud slowly obliterating the sky. Nothing but the purest dream of a new beginning was left between us when she lifted her face to meet my kiss.

11

A week later we returned to the tunnels. We settled in places where they did not know us, where we were strangers. We said nothing about coming from the outside world and told a plausible story about the collapse of our section of the tunnel. That sort of thing happened often.

We kept our secret and awaited the time when we could emerge again, when the green cloud would be gone.

And during that time, as the child grew in her, we made plans. We clarified our ideas. We bided our time. We did not want our child born in the captivity of the tunnels. For her, for him, for us, it would be either freedom or nothing. We knew what kind of future we wanted. It would bear no resemblance to the past.

A year later, we disappeared, and must have been presumed dead. That's what we wanted them to think.

A SHORT INTERVIEW

Why do you think humans have been so irresponsible when making choices related to the future of our planet earth?

People are irresponsible about this because we do not see the immediate evidence of the destruction we are causing, or the effect of that destruction. There is a time gap and even a spatial gap between pollution and the effects of global warming. Also, we don't think that our local actions, the fumes from an industrial plant or from our cars, can possibly affect anything as huge as the global climate. Science has enabled us to see the damage we are causing. Imagination is needed to see how our small causes have global effects.

So many Africans are unaware of the dangers related to climate change, even though many parts of Africa are suffering from desertification and massive pollution. How can one raise awareness of climate change across Africa?

One can raise awareness in Africa through education, online information, protests, stories, folktales, films, television, art, dances, etc. We need continent-wide campaigns. We need local ones too. The voices of the young need to be heard. We need to make environmental sustainability a cultural and social priority. Africa will suffer most from the effects of climate change. Whole portions of the continent could be uninhabitable because of rising temperatures and desertification. Though Africa is responsible for less than ten per cent of global emissions, Africa still needs to play its part in dealing with the problem. Africa can't just leave it to the Western nations. I know we have urgent problems of our own, but climate change ought to be high up in our concern.

Can you explain what you see in what you call the natural tendency of the earth towards balance and harmony?

For every cause there is an effect. Nature is a dynamic system. Energy is constant in the universe. If you heat water, the water doesn't disappear. It becomes air, then forms condensation, then returns to its condition as water. Whatever we do to nature, nature responds, absorbs, adjusts. You pour chemicals into it and chemical reactions occur, and when these come in contact with living beings they suffer the consequences of that chemical action. Our seas are polluted by the gases we emit, and these contaminate marine life. Then marine life suffers, and we have fewer fish. Nature adjusts, but we suffer the form that adjustment takes. Nature strives to maintain its equilibrium, its balance. When we spit at nature, the spit flies back in our face, or in the faces of our children. Nature doesn't do it with intent. If you throw a big stone in a lake, water flies everywhere. It is not directed at you, but this scattering is the response of water to violent displacement. Nature is neutral. It follows its own laws. If we transgress those laws, we suffer. Or generations to come will. And the generations to come will be shocked at our stupidity, our irresponsibility, our lack of vision. Even now we are destroying life on this planet for unborn generations, who will curse us from beyond. So we must act now to save the future.

THE DEVIL'S FUEL

or

I SING THE DAWN OF

BRIGHT, FRESH ENERGY

1

It lives beneath the earth.
Mass of ancient power
Coiled, vast and dark;
A part of the earth's form,
Compressing all that's dead.
Changing like the stars.
Mineralized potential.

And then we smash
The earth's surface to bring
This silent power up
Through water and fire,
From a stillness
That's turned
Old bones and trees
Into fuel and fumes.

It's poisoning the air
Thinning the ecosphere
Destroying lungs
In the world's most
Inefficient way of making
Time turn the wheels
Of a civilization,

Dying because
All that it does
Contributes to its death.

2

They destroy the delta,
Drilling for oil.
They ruin rivers,
Smother forests.
And they uproot
Whole tribes
Dredging up the
Devil's fuel
That every day
Devastates our
Future.

See, the pedal
Of the car drives
That much of our
Lives away.
Our flying through
The air sends us
Faster to the end
We fear.
Our ships that sail
Polluted seas

Sail with us to
Time's darkened lees.

We're chained to it
Like slaves,
Addicts to some
Self-devouring
Drug. We can't seem
To find another way
To make our societies
Work but through this
Form of energy that's
Murdering us
Each hour.

3

It is a strange vision
Of the human race
To build its life
On that which will
Not last.

It's running out
Beneath the earth.
It's running out.
A finite form
Of energy.

But we can now
Make metal out
Of plants
Make energy
From thought
We can power
Our industries
With dreams
We can lift our
Civilization with
The sun
We are made so
That wondrous things
Are done.
We are not prisoners
Of the earth
Manacled to lower
Forms of power,
While the earth is
Cleansed, lashed,
With the rage of the tides
The fury of the storms
The godlike streaks
Of electricity
The ceaseless rush
Of wind.
We live in tornadoes
Of energy
Our earth's ringed with
Electromagnetic
Pulses

In our own way
We are home to
Vast energies
Of the universe.
But poverty of heart
And imagination
Stops us seeing
That we should long ago
Have gone beyond
The primitive
Phase of fossil fuel
And entered the nobler
Stage of solar
Power. We've more
Energy than
We can use in
A million years.

No need to mine
The liquidized
Bones of the dead
No need to use
The dead to drive
Us backwards. No
Need to bring them
Into our air
No need to live
Off death when we
Can live on light.

4

We should swivel
Our technological
Imagination upwards, lift
Our hopes
Towards the sun.
Use what is infinite.
Time will come when
Like fabled civilizations
We will use the power
Of thought to move
With might
The world's machines
Force of soul will
Keep aeroplanes aloft
We'll cook with less
Motion of thought
Than is needed
To tell a lie
They say photons
And neutrinos
Rain down on us
And that a drop
Of water has
Enough power
To light up the
Planet.

We are inefficient
With our ideas
Our possibilities
And our visions.

Our planet is
A magnified
Debris of stars
And we are the
Branches
And filaments
Of the cosmic
Yet we live like
Orphans
Beggars
Paupers
In the universe
When we
Ought to be kings
And queens
Of infinite
Domains.

5

A stone can give
The light of stars
A seed can feed
Hamlets
A thought can raise
Humanity
Out of its self-
Destroying age.

For the age of fossil
Fuels, empires,
And inequalities
Is dead.
Let the dead dream
The dead.

Save the future
Heal the present
Freshen the air
Let the fishes
Breed in peace
In the oceans
Let the rivers
Flow unpolluted with
Mercury, with oil slicks,
With slag and poisons
From industries.

Let the earth breathe
And the topsoil
Be rich again
Free from fertilizers
That make plants grow
Beyond
Their normal speed
And form.
No longer force
Feed pigs
Chickens
And cows.

Let's give our lungs
Pure air to breathe
(Why are exhaust
Pipes of cars at
The level of children
So they breathe in
Directly those
Fresh, murderous
Gases?)
And no longer torture
Our bodies with
Treacherous chemicals
In food we eat
And ambiguous
Fluorides
In our drinking water.

6

I miss the old
Clean taste
Of oranges
I miss breathing
Air without fumes,
Without hydrocarbons.
These pollutions
Have been altering us
And degrading
Our flesh,
Our hearts,
Our spines.
We live longer
But suffer more
Diseases. There're
More sicknesses
Among us now.
I miss clean streams
Without sewage
From our water corporations
I miss rivers
So clear you can
See stones
On their watery beds
And fishes with
Their bright
Gills hovering

In the cool clean
Currents
I miss air so
Pure that every
Breath feels
Like paradise
I miss the taste
Of food that's so
Good it returns
To you your lost
Childhood.
I miss long walks
That don't sicken
You with the carbon dioxide
You breathe unknown
I miss the clear
Blue of the sky.
Our world is being
Powered
By death.
Energy can
Be as harmless
As dreaming trees.

We have not yet
Reached the
True potential
Of the human.
We stand with our
Feet still in

The old kingdom
Of Hades, where
The long dead trees
And bones
Of mammoth beings
Hold up
The foundations
Of our children's
World. We're neck deep
In the oil slime
Of Western civilization.
We are mouth deep
In detritus
We're sleepwalking
In suits and skirts.
Daily the dead
Rise to
Take our places.

The fossil fuel
Revolution
Has been making
The planet mad
Plants are screaming
The sycamore
Tree cries
For eternal
Cleansing
Even the rain
Is contaminated

Falling
Through an
Atmosphere that's
Saturated with
The toxic junk
Of the living.

7

And I said to
The earth, be still.
Yield up no more
Dead force
That's trapped
In coal
Or oil
Or cinnabar
Or magnesium
Or asbestos
Or cobalt
Or tantalum
Or lithium.

And I said to
The sun, teach us
To utilize
Those endless rays

That have open
Hands at their tips
Bring us
Cosmic
Bounty.

And I said to
The wind,
Turn the turbines;
And to the tides,
Speed up the wheels;
And again to the sun
That spreads
Its gold over
The vast unused
Deserts,
Burn away our
Illusions, our sickness
Of heart that makes
Us cultivate
Death in our industries
Unleash
The innocent
Imagination that we may
Draw paradise
Closer
With the work of our hands
And the new century
Of our inventions.

And I said to
Our gardens, spread
Flowers over
The rich deadlands
Of our dried thoughts
Send the fragrance
Of meadows through
The sleep
Of our children
And teach
Our leaders to
Will calm
Splendors
Better realities
For our
Destructive times.

Coral reefs will
Fill with color
Underwater
Kingdoms.
Fishes in the
Panoramas of light
Will bloom again
Where Atlantis
Muses.
Cars will travel
Through the blue air
Houses will be
Lit with our dreams.

I sing the spirit fantastic
I sing the death
Of fossil fuels
I sing a new
Dawning of bright
Fresh energy.

The rivers sing
With me, along
With the voices
Of children in
The everyday
Garden of our
New lives

EXISTENTIAL CREATIVITY

Faced with the state of the world and the depth of denial, faced with the data that keeps falling on us, faced with the sense that we are on a ship heading towards an abyss while the party on board gets louder and louder, I have found it necessary to develop an attitude and a mode of writing that I refer to as existential creativity. This is the creativity at the end of time.

It is not given to many people to sense the end of time approaching. Maybe some Atlanteans sensed it. Maybe the sages of Pompeii, if there were any, felt it in advance. Maybe those ancient civilizations whose societies were about to be wrecked by invaders from the sea felt it. But I can't think of any who had the data indicating that it was coming, who had the facts pouring at them every day, and who carried on as if everything were normal.

Camus writing during the Second World War felt the need for a new philosophy to answer the extreme truths of the times. The absurd was born from that. Existentialism was born too from a world in the throes of extreme crisis. But here we are on the edge of the biggest crisis that has ever faced us. We need a new philosophy for these times, for this near terminal moment in the history of the human being.

It is out of this I want to propose an existential creativity. How do I define it? It is the creativity wherein nothing should be wasted. As a writer, it means everything I write should be directed to the immediate end of drawing attention to the dire position we are in as a species. It means that the writing must have no frills. It should speak only truth. In it the truth must also be beauty. It calls for the highest economy. It means that everything I do must have a singular purpose. It also means that I must write now as if these are the last things I will write, that any of us will write. If you knew you were at the last days of the human story, what would you write? How would you write? What would your aesthetics be? Would you use more words than necessary? What form would poetry truly take? And what would happen to humor? Would we be able to laugh with the sense of the last days upon us?

Sometimes I think we must be able to imagine the end of things, so that we can imagine how we will come through that which we imagine. Of the things that trouble me most, the human inability to imagine its end ranks very high. It means that there is something in the human make-up resistant to terminal contemplation. How else can one explain the refusal of ordinary, good-hearted citizens to face the realities of climate change? If we don't face them, we won't change them. And if we don't change them, we will not put things in motion that would prevent them. And so our refusal to face them will make happen the very thing we don't want to happen.

We have to find a new art and a new psychology to penetrate the apathy and the denial that are preventing governments and corporations from making the changes that are essential if our world is to survive. We need a new art to waken people both to the enormity of what is looming and to the fact that we can still do something about it.

The ability to imagine what we dread most is an evolutionary tool that nature has given us to transcend what we fear. I do not believe that imagining the worst makes it happen. Imagining the worst might be one of the factors that makes us prevent it from happening. That is the function of dystopias and utopias, one to make real to us a destination we must not follow, the other to imagine for us a future that is possible. Fear of poverty has made many people rich. Fear of death has kept many people healthy and sensible in how they live.

There is a time for hope and there is a time for realism. But what is needed now is beyond hope and realism. This is a time when we ought to dedicate ourselves to bringing about the greatest shift in human consciousness and in the way we live. We ought to consecrate ourselves to bringing about a conscious evolutionary leap forward. No longer can we be the human beings we have been, wasteful, thoughtless, selfish, destructive. It is now time for us to be the most creative we have ever been, the most farsighted, the most practical, the most conscious and selfless. The stakes have never been and will never be higher.

What is called for here is a special kind of love for the world, the love of those who discover the sublime value of life because they are about to lose it. For we are on the verge of losing this most precious and beautiful of worlds, a miracle in all the universe, a home for the evolution of souls, a little paradise here in the richness of space, where we are meant to live and grow and be happy, but which we are day by day turning into a barren stone in space.

So a new existentialism is called for. Not the existentialism of Camus and Sartre, negative and stoical in spirit, but a brave and visionary existentialism where, as artists, we dedicate our lives to nothing short of re-dreaming society. We have to be strong dreamers. We have to ask unthinkable questions. We have to go right to the roots of what makes us such a devouring species, overly competitive, conquest-driven, hierarchical.

We ought to ask questions about money, power, hunger. The scientists tell us that fundamentally there is enough for everyone. This earth can sustain us. We can't just ask the shallow questions anymore. Our whys ought to go to the core of what we are. Then we ought to set about changing ourselves. We ought to remake ourselves. Somehow civilization has taken a wrong turn and we need collectively to alter our destination, our journey. We can't drive ourselves to the brink of extinction a second time. If we are to survive this crisis, if we are to pull ourselves back from this waiting apocalypse, then we have to find a global direction of sustenance and justice and beauty for the whole earth, and for all the peoples of the earth.

This is the best and most natural home we are ever going to have. And we need to become a new people to deserve it. We are going to have to be new artists to re-dream it. This is why I propose existential creativity to serve the unavoidable truth of our times and a visionary existentialism to serve the future that we must bring about from the brink of our environmental catastrophe.

We can only make a future from the depth of the truth we face now.

THE SECRET SOURCE

One morning, Fisher discovered that something had been done to the water. For a long while, many people had been saying that there was something different about the water, but no one had really believed them. These claims were seen as just the latest wild rumors emerging from the confused state of the country.

Slowly, the city had been sinking. Its shores were overrun by mice. The foundations of churches were crowded with rats. They could be seen coming out of the graves in broad daylight. Towers had fallen. The streets were potholed and broken. Buses were parked at roadsides. Some of them had been flipped on their sides, and many of them were burntout shells.

Over the course of the previous few days, voices on the radio had been fading away. A sense of exhaustion oozed through the bland tones of the announcers. The government carried on as if nothing unusual were happening, but the prime minister spoke in Parliament of "the enemies within." This sinister phrase set a blaze among the populace. People began to stare at one another in search of signs of this enemy within. Those who looked different naturally qualified more easily for this epithet. There were random attacks in the streets, and the homes of those who seemed to qualify as enemies within were set on fire. Then vigilante gangs rose up in neighborhoods. The police seemed powerless to do anything, as poor government funding had decimated their ranks and public trust in their roles had eroded irredeemably.

Workers went on strike to protest the high cost of water. It seemed to have gone up dramatically overnight. In fact, it had been going up steadily but no one had noticed. No one quite knew why the cost of water had risen so precipitously. For a long time now, the water companies had been dumping sewage back into the nation's waterways. People who went swimming caught disquieting diseases. And because the cost of water had gone up, all the other costs went up too. The truth is that there was a worldwide water shortage. Nations that controlled the world's rivers saw their economic potential. The oceans had become so polluted that the fish caught there poisoned those who ate them. To make things worse, there had not been much rain. Suddenly, water was in short supply.

What was previously an ordinary commodity, a thing that people regularly wasted in baths and decorative fountains in the squares, was now rationed to the point where it was as expensive as gold.

Every household was allowed only fifteen minutes of water each day. The taps ran for that length of time and then stopped. Squabbles and fights over the use of water were common. People were mugged not for their mobile phones but for their bottles of water. In most households, people learned to compress their bodily needs to an extraordinary degree of efficiency. They showered in less than a minute. They cleaned their teeth with a tablespoon of water. Where previously cooking had involved much pouring out of water and juices, now every drop was reused with remarkable creativity.

But Fisher, and the group of school friends with whom he shared a flat on the edge of a council estate, had noticed over the last months that people were changing. Unlike most of his flatmates, Fisher, who lived in the flat with his girlfriend, a carer, didn't have a steady job. He made money doing freelance graphic design and writing articles for newspapers. He spent the rest of his time observing.

He had noticed that the people around him had become docile, amenable to all suggestions from the government. Even radical journalists seemed to be unusually sympathetic to the most extreme government notions. The opposition parties did not oppose anything. The unions capitulated to conditions not even demanded by the companies they worked for. Firebrand activists and comedians began spewing sentimental statements of alarming conservatism. In the midst of all this, the prime minister was often seen smiling. In a recent statement he had said, "It seems we are becoming a nation with a remarkable convergence of views. Dissent has all but disappeared."

No one challenged the complacency of that statement.

Fisher was in his room, thinking about all these unusual occurrences. He was holding his last glass of water for the day. He had been unconsciously looking into the water while he thought. In that state where the mind wanders but the eye is focused, he noticed that there was something odd about the water in his glass. It was like water, but at the same time it had a viscid quality to it; it caught the light in a faintly troubling way. He gazed into the water. Then he saw it. He wasn't sure what he saw. But he saw it.

"It's the water!" he said. "They've done something to the water."

He hurried out of his room to seek his girlfriend. She was in the kitchen, watching the last dribbles of water from the tap.

"It's the water!" he cried to her. "They've made it rare, but they've also made it strange."

Under a magnifying glass, they could see curious striations in the liquid. The surface had a quality that suggested that it could be cut. A drop of the water revealed a world. It was with some horror that they drew back from looking. It occurred to them that the water wasn't really water. It was some kind of simulacrum, virtually indistinguishable from normal water. When they rubbed it between their fingers, the liquid had a faint slipperiness. There was something altogether too finished, too real about it.

Later that evening the friends gathered to discuss what should be done about their discovery. They agreed that they should consult an expert and have the water tested, but realized that they could not trust any such expert. He or she might turn them in. They racked their brains, but could think of no one they knew who could carry out a thorough analysis without drawing the attention of the authorities. Their discussion made clear a number of things. They could no longer trust the water they had been drinking. They saw an immediate correlation between the change in the behavior of the populace and the change in the water.

They did not know when the water had been changed. But they knew that it had been this way for some time, because when they looked back they understood that they had all been more passive and less inclined to question anything for a while now.

"There are two things we need to do," Fisher said.

"Get the water analyzed," said his girlfriend, Venus.

"And stop drinking it," said one of the flatmates.

"That means one crucial thing," Fisher said.

"What?"

"We have to find water that hasn't been corrupted."

"How will we do that?"

"I don't know. We need water to live. Without it, we will surely die. The question is whether we go on drinking this water that is doing things to us that we don't know about, perhaps turning us into morons, or whether we find water that's untouched, that's pure."

They talked deep into the night. At first they thought they could somehow carry on as normal. Then they realized that their discovery had marked a turning point in their lives. They had to do something. They decided that they would live off the water in fruit. They would wash the fruit with tap water, but they would not drink it. They knew that they only had a number of days, after which they would begin to suffer the ill effects of not drinking enough water. One set of friends would take on the task of getting the water analyzed. The other set would take on the task of finding new water. They drew lots. The task of finding new water fell to Fisher and Venus. They went to sleep that night exhausted but clear in their minds for the first time in months.

*

In the morning, they dispersed. The agreement was that they would converge at the flat after a week. If anything happened, they would abort the meeting. If any one of them was killed, the others would have to make their own way and try to convey their findings to the rest of society, provided there was anyone left to listen.

Those meant to have the water analyzed set out first. They made for the university. They kept in touch through coded texts on their mobile phones. It all went well until they arrived at the university and met a member of the chemistry faculty who agreed to perform tests. The tests were being carried out, and some findings were about to come in when the coded messages ceased. Then all went silent.

Late in the morning, it became clear to Fisher and Venus that they had to begin their quest and that their flat might not be safe anymore. They took some essentials and traveled light. They had no idea where to go. They went to visit friends on the rich side of town. The friends found their story and their suspicions ridiculous. From a top-floor window Fisher spotted policemen approaching the house. He alerted Venus and they escaped through a back door and made their way through gardens and over fences. They left town. They visited relatives and soon realized that they were somehow expected wherever they turned up. So they avoided all the people they knew and decided instead to plunge below the surface of society. They changed their clothes and altered their appearance and disappeared.

They found themselves with drug dealers and lived rough with the homeless. They felt safe with the homeless. But there was a drought in the city. The great river flowed stodgily. Buckets and plastic bags and mattresses and garbage and fishing nets in which sea creatures were entangled could be seen floating on the river, along with suspicious-looking substances of an indeterminate color. At night, in the streets, people sold water at high prices. They had barrels and buckets and plastic bottles of water. They wore masks because they did not want to be recognized by the many cameras that gazed at them from streetlamps and the edges of buildings. People came out of their houses or furtively out of cars to buy water and then ran back to anonymity again. Fisher bought a bottle of water but one look showed that it was not fit to drink. The water was striated with wavy lines. Tiny globular dots could be seen with a magnifying glass.

Fisher and Venus drifted with the hordes of the homeless. Among them were those who had chosen to be homeless, who lived underground to escape the traps of modern life. They lived in tents in fields at night, or along the canals. The sanest among them drank no water, and their eyes shone with defiance; they spoke little and were suspicious of everyone. It was from them that Fisher learned that there were people who were making alternative water. They had their own mobile chemical operations and they distilled water from rainfall. Fisher sought out these distillers, searching through a warren of dim houses on the edge of the city. They were a cautious lot, for they had been infiltrated often by the government and lost many colleagues. They changed their accommodation nightly. Fisher and Venus came with recommendations and passed the lie-detector tests, but Fisher found the water they were processing to be no good. Though it appeared to be natural rainfall, it was nonetheless contaminated. This discovery was very upsetting to the secretive water-distillers. They threw Fisher and Venus out, accusing them of being saboteurs.

"We're not saboteurs," Venus cried. "We're just trying to find the truth, like you, that's all. But even nature has been corrupted."

The water-distillers were no longer listening. They had spirited themselves away to another secret location. Fisher and Venus had no choice but to make their way back into the city. On the way, Fisher noticed a small headline on a sheet of newspaper that had been discarded in the street. For a long time now, their generation had stopped reading the newspapers or trusting them, as they were almost all owned by billionaires who had their own secret agendas. The papers that were independent were all edited and run by people who had gone to elite schools and universities where the education had long been tainted by the prevailing orthodoxies. There was only so much truth they could tell and, besides, they took their instructions covertly from the government, who insisted that the nation was in a state of siege. The news Fisher and Venus's generation relied on came from underground sources, whispers, legends, things passed on and sifted by people they could trust, who were not paid and had no personal or political agendas. Nonetheless the headline caught Fisher's eye.

"Look at this!" he said.

They read it together. There was only half of the article left. The other half had been torn by the wind.

"The Water Wars," it read. "Now fully half the world is engaged in water wars. The other half has no water. Cities around the world are perishing of thirst. Where has all the water g—"

There was nothing else.

"So, it's global," Venus said.

"Maybe. I wouldn't trust that fragment."

They sat by the roadside. They were weary. They hadn't drunk water in four days. After a short rest, they continued walking. They sought out healers. But the healers they found had venal eyes. One of them made insinuations to Venus. Another claimed to have the best water in the world, but when she brought it out Venus nearly fainted at its color. It was pitch-black. It gleamed like mercury, and it tasted like water. It was the weirdest thing they'd ever seen.

"I think I'm beginning to hallucinate," Venus said. "What was that?"

They were back out in the street. Venus had lost her mobile phone. She was sure the last healer they'd gone to had stolen it. They thought, after that, that they should maybe try scientists again. They had had enough of unreason. They caught a ride to Venus's old university and sought out her former chemistry lecturer. They found him in his office. He had a few tufts of hair on his head but had copious hair in his nostrils and on the back of his neck. He looked old and a bit tired and there was no animation in his eyes when he saw Venus.

"I remember you," he said. "It's Venus, isn't it? You were the prettiest girl in the whole university, did you know that? We all considered it a special privilege to have you in our class. What can I do for you?"

After the initial discomfiture produced by his remark, they told him. He listened to them with his eyes shut. When they finished, he sighed.

"It seems," he said, "that I failed to convey to you the most fundamental tenet of science. And that is rationality. You must follow the facts. Don't deviate from them. Your emotions are not important in science. Nor are your political views. Just the facts. Now why would anyone wish to tamper with the water? If it is, as you say, to create in the populace a certain uniformity of thought, how could this be achieved? I really don't see how drinking water can alter your politics or temper your passions."

"But there are drugs designed to tranquilize. We use them for schizophrenia, manic depression…"

"Are you suggesting that the government…? That is too absurd. It is unscientific."

"What about the analysis of the water, the floating dots?"

"Water has never been pure. For thousands of years we have managed with impure water. It is only in the last hundred years that we have had the technology to refine it. Refining is not contaminating. Where did you get that idea?"

Venus and Fisher listened to him in controlled astonishment. It was as though he were addressing not them but their whole generation. He had some kind of grudge and they were bearing the brunt of it. As he spoke he got up and fetched himself a large glass of water from the tap. He drank it while watching them.

"I drink this water all the time and there has never been anything wrong with my mental processes. In fact, they get sharper every day. This year alone, I have made five new discoveries which prove that most of the assertions of the environmental movement are claptrap. There is no global warming. The forests of the earth are doing just fine. There is absolutely no proof of a diminishment of any of the species. I keep being nominated for the Nobel Prize, so there," he said, and drank what was left in the glass.

They thanked him for his time and hurried out. They had just left the campus when a police van arrived. They plunged back into the substrata of the city. In their wanderings, they met people who claimed never to have drunk tap water in their lives. Some showed the youthfulness of their skins as proof. One of them was a Rastafarian who said he was a hundred years old and had lived so long because he had avoided all the corruptions of the system.

"I see what dem do to the water," he said.

Upon further questioning, it turned out that he had not really witnessed anything. He was referring dimly to some second sight. Also, he was fuzzy about his age. Their inference put it at about eighty. But this was still impressive, given his evident vigor.

They met people who had heard rumors of good water. They were sent to many places, to many people. They met a seer, a wise woman, a psychic, a doctor, a philosopher. But none of them had any notion of where the good water could be found.

"To question the water you drink," the philosopher said, "is to question the very fundamentals of the society you live in. It is like questioning the air you breathe."

"But some do exactly that," Venus said.

"It is not wise to doubt your reality," the philosopher said. "Because there is no other."

"Is that true?" Fisher asked.

"I fear," the philosopher said, not hearing him, "that you have left yourselves out on a limb. You've cut the ground from beneath you. It is an unsustainable philosophical position. The water is good and has always been good. The next thing you'll doubt is life itself, which is a very sure way to exit it."

With that the philosopher dismissed them and took a sip from his tall, thin glass of water.

They had now gone seven days without drinking water, surviving on only the liquid from fruits. They felt as if their brains were shrinking. Even bottled water that supposedly came from pristine streams and lakes in the mountains had the same peculiar striations, the same barely visible whorls. This anomalous condition of water was universal. Fisher claimed that he was now officially hallucinating. He saw pools of pure water in the road. Venus saw fountains sprouting out of concrete. They became so parched that they finally agreed their course of action had been insane.

"You can't go against the world," Fisher said, hardly getting his words out.

Almost fainting, they leaned against each other. They shut their eyes and succumbed to oblivion. Then a child came to them.

"What are you doing?" he asked.

"We were looking for good water we can drink," Fisher said.

"But now we have given up. Such water does not exist," said Venus.

"I know someone who has the best water in the world," the boy said brightly.

"Who?"

Venus and Fisher opened their eyes.

"My grandfather."

"Can you take us to him?"

"Yes, of course."

The boy led them to an opening in the earth and down stone steps into the dark depths. They went down for a long time. Sometimes the steps became winding and they descended in a spiral. It was very dark and hot. The child had no light.

"Is it safe down here?" Venus asked.

"Very."

"Is it far to go?" Fisher asked.

"Very."

They could not see the steps now, but they felt them. The walls were rough. They went down for what seemed like hours.

"Who is your grandfather?" Fisher asked.

"Few people know."

"How did he come by the water?" Venus asked.

"It was always there."

"But why didn't he share it?"

"He did, but people didn't want it. They wanted the one that's killing them."

Venus suddenly buckled. Fisher caught her. She was afraid and refused to go any farther.

"It wasn't an accident that I found you," the child said. "We heard that you were looking for this water. You are the only ones who have sought this water in a long time. You would never have found it yourselves."

"Why not?"

"The water has to find you."

Then the child gave Venus something to drink in the dark and she felt stronger.

"That's the loveliest water I have tasted in my life," she said.

They resumed their descent. It became increasingly hard for Fisher to breathe. His legs were still strong, but his mind gave way. He began to topple over, but Venus caught him and helped him to sit on the stone step. He was gasping for air, like a beached fish.

"I can't go on," he said. "Just leave me here to die."

Then the child gave Fisher something to drink in the darkness, and he felt stronger. The air became cool and reviving. He could faintly make out the steps in the catacomb blackness. He noticed that Venus's eyes were shining.

They continued their descent. They could no longer hear their footfalls or the echo of their breathing. They became aware that the boy was no longer with them. There was only a faint white light ahead. Then they reached it.

There was a clearing. An old man was seated on a stone chair. Behind him, something shone with an unnatural light. That was what had lit up the dark.

"What is that?" they asked the man.

"That," he said, "is the last real water left in the world."

SOME MYSTERIOUS FORCE

Nature is beautiful
Can't be denied.
Do we know why?
Mahogany trees in
Teeming forests
English elms whispering
In the meadows
The Gulf of Naples the color
Of green diamonds
Sunlight glimmering on the grass
Cornfields in the moonlight
The misty crown of blue mountains
Waterfalls they call the tears of a god
Some unknown force behind it all

The emperor penguins
Fading from view
The piano-playing spiders
Juggling dolphins
Long-flying birds
Hovering bees
Outsider foxes and
Sarcastic wolves
Schools of fishes
That turn and dart
Together in telepathic motion
Fishes that leap

And contemplate the land
A moment and then reject it
Oaks that grow diagonally
On the side of a hill
Some mysterious power behind it all

What do we know
Of the wonder of the dragonfly
Or the intelligence of the dog?
The earth responds
With invisible nerves
To everything we do.
A sweet energy runs
Through the sap of a tree
And shows itself off in the rose,
Hibiscus and the daffodils.

Long before we stood on two legs
Earth had a replete destiny.
She helped us to stand straight
And her food nourished our
Tentative myths.
She already contained the secret
Of fire folded in stones.
Future ships and rockets
And space stations
And computers
And phones were already
Implied in the gleam of light
Which rainfall reveals on high rocks.
She had all our future before

Whatever chance or miracle brought us
Out of the womb of sea or land.
The first music was hers.
She made rock paintings long
Before rocks were painted.
The future is not really ours but hers
And like trees we will listen to the wind.

Roots run deep in the busy earth
And they speak a subterranean language.
I can show you magic in a handful of soil.
Mushrooms have their mute lexicons
Great rivers like the Amazon
Are the serpent power of the world
And oceans have their encyclopedias.
A small fox in the undergrowth
Made me jump at its big presence
In our narrowing world.
Some unseen radiance behind it all.

ANTHEM

Can't you hear the
Future weeping?

Our love must save
The world

Can't you hear us
Future fighting
We are the hope
Of the world

We will rise
And we will dream

We heal her
And keep her strong

How can we turn
Our times around

We must fight for
This world that we love

But can you hear
The future weeping?

Our love must
Save the world.